Alice in the Wasteland

Contents

DESCENT INTO MADNESS	7
ABYSS OF TEARS	17
RAT RACE	27
RABBIT STEW	35
CRACKED-OUT TAPEWORM	49
PIG ROAST	61
MOCHA FRAPPUCINO	75
ROYAL RUMBLE	91
TURTLE SOUP	107
LOWER THE SEWER LOBSTER	121
INJUSTICE SYSTEM	133
THE FINAL VERDICT	145

CHAPTER 1
DESCENT INTO MADNESS

Amidst the barren wastelands, where ash-ridden skies bled gray, Alice sat wearied beside the skeletal remains of what she believed was her mother. It was difficult to distinguish a trace of her long-lifeless form amidst the scorched earth. An old tome lay next to the scattered bone fragments, its pages parched and weathered, devoid of illustrations or text. "What's the worth of a book," Alice pondered, "in a world where voices have been silenced and visions perished?"

Beneath the harsh glare of what might be her final sunset, Alice contemplated through the haze of her dehydrated thoughts. Might the fleeting joy of chaining mutated daisies into a necklace outweigh the risk of standing and exposing herself to the predators?

Just then, through the swirling dust, a gaunt rabbit, its eyes bleeding pink from the radiation, staggered past.

In any other setting, a talking rabbit would be the sign of mental breakdown. But here, amidst the end of days, Alice merely tilted her head when it muttered, "I'm late. Doomed to be dismembered, my severed feet made into good luck charms. As if there were such a thing as good luck in this forsaken hell."

The suffering creature momentarily stopped wringing its inexplicably white-gloved paws. It pulled a shattered, rusted pocketwatch from its tattered vest. Alice's suppressed curiosity ignited. In a realm where time had ceased its march, a creature bound by a deadline was a mystery she could not resist. She trailed the emaciated mammal as it vanished into an immense crevice beneath a withered row of genetically modified corn.

Perversely overcome with an urge to plumb the depths of this burgeoning insanity, and without a moment's pause or reflection on her own survival due to the unyielding trauma of the wasteland, she followed, staggering zombie-like into the abyss below.

Suddenly, Alice was in freefall, physically and mentally. The pit seemed to stretch endlessly like an abandoned cosmic mine shaft. Down and down she spiraled, time seeming to stand still and rush violently forward all at once. In the dim, bioluminescent glow, she glimpsed shelves marked "IKEA", poorly installed into the earthen walls, laden with decomposing remnants of eras yet to come. Maggot-infested Chicken McNuggets, camouflage Crocs, intercontinental ballistic missiles and, bizarrely, a moldy plastic bottle labeled "PRIME HYDRATION STRAWBERRY WATERMELON BY LOGAN PAUL". To her dismay, the putrid container held only tainted echoes of sweetness. In the throes of obsessive-compulsive disorder, she felt compelled to place it back on the shelf, but thought better of it. Perhaps it would fall into the hands of someone who knew where the recycling bin was. Yet what was the point of recycling when less than 10% of materials disposed this way were actually reclaimed?

"In this mad world torn asunder," Alice mused, "jumping into this dark portal may be the sanest act I've ever committed. Those who lurk in the shadows of the surface would call me a legend. Ending another human's life in order to survive will seem a child's play after this."

Deeper still she went. The void seemed eternal. She wondered aloud, her voice echoing eerily, "How far have I delved? Far enough to be consumed by lakes of molten iron beneath the Earth's fouled crust?" Might I descend straight into the realm of the damned? Into the dominion of cursed souls?" The thought dizzied her addled brain and sent shivers down her spine.

As she spiraled into the seemingly infinite emptiness, the mournful cry of Dienah, her abandoned pet cat, echoed in her mind. "Tonight, she wanders the ruins alone, seeking that last vestige of rancid milk."

Her mind began to wander to the hellscape's grotesque vampire bats with eyes that gleamed malevolently. She wondered: Do cats dare challenge such bats?" The chilling thought threatened to drag her into madness, "Bats and cats, cats and bats," until a bone-jarring crash halted her descent, depositing her amongst a large pile of used diabetes test strips and Narcan applicators.

With a frantic heartbeat, Alice scanned the haunting expanse and gasped. The ghostly figure of the gaunt rabbit appeared in the abyss and muttered, "Time's curse tightens its grip." Alice was chilled to the core, but she pursued the rabbit instinctively. She tailed it into a vast cavern, lit only by sickly glowing fungi that seemed to whisper secrets of the dead.

Doors, smeared with symbols of forgotten rituals, barricaded her path. Their silent rebuke intensified her dread. Stumbling upon an obsidian table, she found a small, tarnished golden key. None of the rough-hewn doors yielded to it. But a hidden recess revealed a tiny door, beyond which lay a garden, unnaturally alive amidst encircling death, its plants writhing as if possessed. As she poked her head in, Alice felt the plants telepathically taunting her as she struggled unsuccessfully to fit her body through the small opening.

"Perhaps if my head were now decapitated," Alice thought, "I would experience a brief respite as it rolled away."

Her tone was not sarcastic but practical. So many

horrifyingly impossible things had happened already, it wasn't difficult to imagine that her head detaching from her body would be more relieving than traumatizing.

Alice was defeated but desperate to reach the presumed safety of the garden, to the extent the wasteland had not rendered the idea of safety entirely foreign. She returned to the table looking for something sharp. Instead, she noticed a vial on the table, bearing the label, "DRINK ME (HOUSEMADE ORGANIC NON-GMO FAIR TRADE)". It had not been there before. Alice was less surprised from its unexplainable appearance than her irrational and immediate urge to quaff the mystery liquid.

The absence of a poison mark on the vial tempted her further, but in this realm, even the most innocent-looking elixirs could be expected to unleash unspeakable horrors. Memories of dreadful tales from the apocalyptic surface cycled obsessively in her mind, tragic visions of souls ensnared by temptation.

Alice cautiously sniffed the bottle. The amalgam of flavors—like fragrant remnants of a world eternally consumed—proved too alluring, and she succumbed, drinking deeply.

The liquid inside was black and had a gritty texture as it passed over her lips. Amidst overpowering sensations of nausea and disgust, Alice's thoughts escaped inward. "Is this reality or a shattered fragment of my imagination?" she mused, attempting to grapple with the surreal transformations. "Perhaps I'm ensnared within the illusions of my own psyche." Her dissociation did well to swallow the potion without vomiting.

In the muted gloom, Alice felt a dissonance enveloping her being. "This unsettling feeling," she whispered, "is akin to folding inward, like the collapsing of a black hole."

A high-pitched noise suddenly rose to a deafening roar. Alice trembled with panic as her legs and arms rapidly began to lose their length. She felt horrifying discomfort as her internal organs shrunk and squeezed together, aghast as the world around her grew more imposing every moment. In seconds, the bewildering transformation was complete. There was no denying it: Alice was now mere inches in height, a small and vulnerable creature in a world of predatory horrors. Her stature now mirrored the diminished remnants of the world around her, standing but a mere fragment of her former self.

She came to what little was left of her senses. The prospect of wandering through the doorway into that long-forgotten oasis of muted greenery ignited a glimmer of hope in her eyes. Yet, she hesitated, fearing she might continue to diminish, dissipating into nothingness. "Would I fade," she pondered, "like the dim glow of a snuffed-out wick? Can the essence of a soul echo in the void?"

No further transformation gripped Alice, yet anxiety maintained an excruciating grip on her every nerve. She turned toward the garden. The fates seemed to conspire against her. The golden key, once a symbol of hope and entry, now sat elusive on the tabletop high above, mocking her from atop what seemed a towering monolith. Despair clung to her soul as she struggled to ascend, but the table, slick as the treacheries of the wasteland, denied her ascent. She was left a crumpled heap at its base. Utterly defeated, Alice wept more deeply than she could ever remember weeping before.

"Cease this lament," she chided herself, her voice echoing the sternness of suppressed traumas through mucus-drenched heaves.

Then, amidst the desolation, she spied a relic: a glass container, sheltering a fragment of a bygone era – a cake adorned with the words "DIET EAT ME (CONTAINS ASPARTAME, A KNOWN CARCINOGEN)" hastily arranged in rancid M&M candies. Desperation and hope melded. "Should I swell in size, the key shall be mine; diminish further, and I'll either slip beneath the door or mercifully die in the process," she resolved. "Should I live long enough to suffer from a debilitating illness, I shall consider myself lucky indeed."

Biting into the morsel, she awaited a shift in her being. Yet, to her astonishment, she remained unchanged. Unsettled by the unceasing anomalies, the sudden mundanity of the ordinary seemed a cruel jest. Had she already gone insane, expecting the cake to transform her the way the mysterious liquid did? Alice was not one to relent. She consumed the last of the dessert. Her last dessert?

Alice's diminished stature — a mere ten inches tall — did little to comfort her wavering sanity. The enticement of the garden, a beacon of normality in this lunacy, fortified her will. But as moments passed without further transformation, an unsettling thought intruded: "What if this static state is but a precursor to complete oblivion? Will I dissipate like a fleeting memory, forever lost in an infinite purgatory of nothingness?"

The forsaken key, having been forgotten during the transformation, now sat unreachable. Alice struggled in futility to retrieve it, hindered by her diminutive size and the table's greasy, slippery surface. Tears formed, not solely out of frustration but from an overwhelming dread of her own spiritual disintegration.

"I've been through worse on the surface," Alice muttered to herself. She tied together enough of the fraying threads of her sanity to muster up some semblance of resilience. Surely there must be some way to escape her current situation, even if that escape was necessarily permanent.

Every corner of the hall bore an eerie, distorted visage that gnawed at Alice's tortured soul. Shadows lengthened and danced in unpredictable patterns, their grotesque shapes shifting, threatening to engulf her. The walls seemed to breathe, pulsating to a nightmarish rhythm.

Suddenly, Alice felt her stomach turn and its contents liquify. A burning sensation from deep within her intestines expanded to penetrate every cell of her body, as if each individual strand of DNA was being torn from her being, spooled together and woven into a tapestry of primal suffering. Her skin began to stretch like fabric pulled taut enough to tear. Bone splinters exploded in her limbs as they extended in length. Like cutting an onion in reverse, her face continuously peeled off her skull and was replaced. Her eyeballs bulged, her tongue swelled. She feared the room would not hold her rapid expansion, and her body would simply grow until it imploded under the pressure of her environment.

CHAPTER 2
ABYSS OF TEARS

"Stranger things have happened", Alice intoned sarcastically, grasping at her rapidly deteriorating consciousness in a desperate attempt to see the humor in her situation. There was no laughter. Her voice seemed detached, a phantom echo in the oppressive atmosphere. The unnatural stretching of her body made the world twist and turn in impossible angles. Her feet, once a comforting touch to the ground, seemed miles away, a fading memory of her former self. A chilling thought crossed her mind: "If my own feet become strangers, shall I become detached from the remaining parts of my body? What other horrors await in this fiendish dimension?"

She was shocked back into the surrealist hellscape when her head painfully slammed into the roof, causing her vision to blur. Clinging tenuously to consciousness, she desperately reached for the tarnished golden key, barely grasping it between her sweaty fingers. A shadowy presence, barely discernible, darted past the periphery of her vision. Looking around, disoriented, she managed again to glimpse the garden — a cursed Eden of writhing flora and dark silhouettes. It beckoned and repelled in equal measure.

She plummeted downward into sorrow amidst the hall's chilling, foreign atmosphere. The walls seemed to close in, whispering tales of those who once tread its expanse, now lost forever. Her freakishly oversized tears did not merely flow; they threatened to flood the hall with her despair. She thought drowning in them might be preferable to continuing the nightmare of her existence.

As the cold, salty water lapped against her, Alice felt the weight of the mortifying mutation she'd undergone. All of existence had turned upside down, and now she was marooned in a pool of her own lachrymation, shrinking and growing at the whim of magical liquids and edibles with mysterious labels. She thought of the gaunt rabbit's strange little gloves, the elusive key, and the garden she so desperately wanted to reach. The universe seemed to be playing a cruel joke on her, and she was not amused.

Alice's miserable introspection was interrupted by the sound of calloused feet and overgrown toenails dragging against the floor in the distance. As the scraping sounds echoed, they were accompanied by a cacophony of sinister whispers and murmurs. The sounds grew louder, the words incomprehensible, as if a horde of demonic entities had manifested from hell to mock her plight. The Off-White Rabbit emerged from the darkness, staring blankly ahead.

"Am I not already condemned for my tardiness?" he

asked no one in particular. "Surely the Dutchess will waterboard and electrocute me for such insolence."

Alice contemplated the unreality of the talking rabbit and her freakishly large stature. Madness and doubt seeped into her core, her sense of self dangling precipitously above a chasm of nothingness.

In a desperate bid to recall and anchor herself, she began reciting the things she once knew. But with each mistake, the hall seemed to grow darker, and the shadows more animated. Her own voice became a distorted mockery, echoing back her errors with chilling glee.

Lost in this Byzantine maze of twisted reality, Alice's struggle was not just against the life-threatening changes she underwent, but against the insidious dread of a world determined to pull her into its macabre dance of doom. She had to cling, white-knuckled, to her sense of self, lest she be lost forever in the terrifying void of the unknown. A long-forgotten song came to her lips:

Ice ice baby
Ice ice baby
All right stop, collaborate and listen
Ice is back with a brand new invention
Something grabs a hold of me tightly
Flow like a harpoon daily and nightly
Will it ever stop?

Yo, I don't know
Turn off the lights and I'll glow
To the extreme I rock a mic like a vandal
Light up a stage and wax a chump like a candle

"I'm certain these words are a twisted echo," muttered Alice, her eyes brimming with stinging tears. Somewhere within the recitation of the verse, she had forgotten who or what she was entirely.

"What is my role in this forsaken world? Reveal that first, and only if the identity pleases me, I shall emerge. If not, I'll remain buried here until I morph into yet another entity. But, alas!" wailed Alice, as a surge of tears ruptured forth, "The solitude in this desolate abyss wearies my soul!"

As she spoke these words, Alice cast her gaze upon her trembling hands. To her bewilderment, she had donned one of the Rabbit's tattered white kid gloves during her soliloquy. "How have I come to this?" she pondered. "I must be diminishing once more." Rising, she stumbled to the table, seeking to gauge her dwindling stature against it, and discerned, with a shudder, that she had shriveled to a mere two feet in height. Her mind had wandered so far astray that it disconnected from her body, and Alice hardly noticed she had once again shrunk into vulnerable prey.

"That was a brush with oblivion!" gasped Alice, her heart pounding with terror at the abrupt transformation, yet relieved to still be breathing. "Now, to the forsaken garden!" With frantic haste, she dashed back to the diminutive portal, but, to her despair, it was sealed once more, the diminutive golden key mocking her from atop the glass table, just as before. "The nightmare deepens," mumbled the forlorn child, choking on mucus.

As these words slipped from her chapped lips, her footing betrayed her, and in an instant, splash! She found herself submerged up to her chin in a saline deluge. Her initial thought was that she had plunged into the sea, "and if so, I can retreat by submarine." (Alice had once ventured to the seaside, naively deducing from that singular experience that any English coastal excursion led one to encounter a myriad of bloated bathers bobbing lifeless in the ocean, men in hazmat suits probing eroded sand dunes with Geiger counters, a line of identically constructed – and identically charred – lodging houses, and, observing it all, the crooked periscope of a beached nuclear submarine.) It didn't take long for her to realize that she was both delusional and drowning, marooned in the vast lake of tears she had shed at her previously towering height.

"I regret unleashing such a deluge of my own wastewater!" Alice lamented, paddling desperately in search of an escape. "I'm to be condemned for my own sorrow, destined to drown in a sea of my own moist regrets!"

At that moment, she detected the sound of something thrashing in the water not far off. She considered swimming closer to investigate, but her second thought was of some leviathan – a horrible, tentacled beast of the deep. Then, recalling her diminished size, she soon realized it was but a small and sickly rat, equally victim to the whims of this surreal world, having tumbled into the tearful lake just as she had.

"Is there any point, I wonder," Alice pondered, "in conversing with this rodent? Everything is so bizarre here, it wouldn't surprise me if it could talk. At any rate, attempting won't hurt." Thus, she ventured, "Sieg Heil! Herr Rat, do you know an escape from this watery prison? We can't tread water forever, Herr Rat!" (Alice believed this to be the proper manner of addressing a rat, never having attempted such before, but something about the red armband and dark patch of fur on its lip suggested Germanic fascism.") The Sewer Rat regarded her with a suspicious glance, and appeared to wink slyly with one of its tiny clouded eyes, yet it remained silent.

"Perhaps it's a French fascist," Alice speculated; "It could be a member of the French Popular Party." (With her hazy grasp of history, Alice couldn't quite place the timing of past violence.) So she tried again: "Où est ma chatte?" the opening line of her French textbook. The Sewer Rat, in sheer terror, leapt from the water, shivering violently. "Wait!" Alice exclaimed in haste, fearing she had used the wrong pronoun. "Oh, of course! You're not fond of cats, I suppose. Forgive me, I take it all back."

"Not fond of cats!" the Sewer Rat shrieked in a piercing, fervent voice. "Would you be fond of the mongrels that murdered and slowly ate your family in front of you?"

"My family is also dead," Alice replied in a bitter tone. "Has it not occurred to you that whatever God created this world of cats and mice, forever locked in a game of death, is the one to blame for our suffering? What is the Creator if not an apex predator?"

The Sewer Rat's face contorted in resentful confusion, a high-pitched growl building in its waterlogged lungs.

"I do wish you could have met our cat Dienah", Alice continued, more to herself as she floated aimlessly, shivering in the cold pool. "I believe you might have grown fond of cats if you could have seen her. She was such a gentle soul, always purring so contentedly by the flaming rubble, grooming her paws, cleaning entrails from her face — and she was so soft to hold — and a notorious slayer of rodent vermin — oh, I apologize!" Alice exclaimed again, noticing the Rat now looked thoroughly incensed, its dirty, matted fur somehow standing on end, tiny chipped teeth bared. "We can change the subject."

The Sewer Rat bellowed, quivering from nose to tail tip: "What cruel God would create a creature specifically to torment me and my kind until we are eradicated? There is no God."

"Let's reverse course," Alice declared, eager to divert the conversation. "Do you — perhaps — have any fondness for — dogs? After all, in a way, 'dog' is the opposite of 'God.'"

The Sewer Rat brought its paw to its face and covered its eyes, shaking its head. Alice ignored this, pressing her case: "There's a delightful little dog near our home I'd love for you to see! Well, if he hasn't succumbed to the wasteland, that is. He's a three-legged terrier with long, matted fur. It limps to retrieve thrown objects, begs for its meals when not eating its own feces, and performs all manner of tricks — I can't recall them all — and it's owned by an exterminator, who claims it's so adept at ratting, it's valued at ten million credits! He says it decimates all the rats and — oops." Alice exclaimed remorsefully, "Sorry." The Rat was now fleeing, screeching through the water as fast as it could, stirring the pool into a frenzy.

Alice became desperate. "Don't leave me alone here! I promise no more talk of predation!" Hearing this, the Rat paused, then hesitantly circled back towards her, its countenance ashen (from rage, Alice assumed). In a quavering voice, it proposed, "Only if you come with me. I will show you why you're wrong. You will see why all living things must die."

"A horrifying proposition", Alice thought, but the time was indeed ripe for departure, as the pool was now inexplicably teeming with various diseased birds, malnourished animals and horrifying insects that had tumbled in: a Maggot, a Dodo, a Cockroach, a Tick, and several other peculiar creatures with mutated forms, missing appendages and oozing wounds.

"This is my life now," Alice conceded.

The entire assembly of forgotten and discarded creatures swam towards the shore, following (pursuing?) Alice as she struggled out of the water.

CHAPTER 3
RAT RACE

Upon the bank of the oil-slick sea, they formed an eccentric assemblage: the wretched birds with their feathers sodden and drooping, the diseased animals with their muddy fur plastered to their bodies, macabre insects with drooping wings, all soaked, irritable, and depressed.

The paramount concern, naturally, was finding a means to dry off before hypothermia set in. A desperate scramble for a solution quickly led some of the creatures to convene and chair a council on this matter. Within minutes, Alice found herself conversing with this congress of oddities as though they were old acquaintances. In fact, she engaged in a rather heated debate with the Cockroach, who eventually turned petulant, insisting, "I am older than you, your generation is so lazy;" a point Alice could not concede without knowing its exact age. The Cockroach claimed to have lost its official identification and thus had no proof of birthdate. Alice suspected this to be a lie, but was too exhausted to press the issue further.

Eventually, the Rat, who appeared to be a dictator-like figure in this motley crew, commanded, "Sit down and shut up, all of you! Attend to me! I will make the wasteland dry again!" They promptly formed a menacing circle, seating themselves with the Rat at its center. Alice watched anxiously. She could no longer feel her fingers or toes, and she feared they would require amputation should she remain cold and wet for much longer.

"Listen up!" the Rat began, assuming a grave demeanor, "are you ready to dry off? Everybody shut up and pay attention!" He pulled out a thick stack of paper and began reading aloud.

"This Agreement governs your use of our drying services, through which you can buy, license, rent or subscribe to drying content, drying Apps (as defined below), and other drying services (collectively, 'Drying'). Drying may be offered through the services by Ratco or a third party. Our Services are available for your use in your country or territory of residence ('Home Country'). By creating an account for use of the Drying services in a particular country or territory you are specifying —"

Even in her addled state, Alice quickly surmised the Rat sought to coerce the audience members into a binding contract that undermined their best interests. The creatures appeared to lack the mental capacity to understand this and instead became even more restless as their limbs stiffened under the oppressive cold.

Finally, the Tick spoke up: "Make the wasteland dry again!"

This got a rousing round of hollering and wet-pawed applause from the huddled mass of soggy and sorry creatures, and pretty soon they had formed a mosh pit circle around Alice. It immediately became impossible to see her hand in front of her face as huge volumes of radioactive dust were kicked up, rising to blot out what little sunlight was shining through the sky overhead.

The Dodo pulled itself up on the Tick's exoskeleton and crowd-surfed to an eroded sand dune that formed a makeshift stage on the beach. The circle pit lost its formation and soon the crowd was standing dumbly looking up at the Dodo, appendages crossed.

"Congratulations to all the winners of the race!" the Dodo exclaimed.

The crowd was confused. It hadn't occurred to anyone – Alice included – that they were in a race. A voice from the center called out, "Who won?"

This conundrum left the Dodo lost in contemplation, inhaling deeply on his vape pen and blowing out a massive cloud of grape-scented chemicals. The others stared blankly with mouths agape in hushed anticipation. Finally, the Dodo declared, "Everyone wins. Everyone gets a prize."

"But who shall distribute these prizes?" a chorus of voices inquired eagerly.

"The answer is obvious," the Dodo pronounced, gesturing towards Alice with a dirty, broken wing. The entire assembly swarmed around her, clamoring in a disordered chorus, "Rewards! Rewards!"

Alice, at a loss, rummaged through her pockets in desperation and was surprised to find a small bag labeled "Doritos." Miraculously spared by the salt water, she opened the garish sack and distributed each orange triangular unit as rewards. Though the bag was filled with mostly air, there was miraculously one "Dorito" for each foul being.

"However, she herself must also receive a reward," the Rat interjected.

"No cap," the Dodo concurred with solemnity. "What else you got in those pockets?" it demanded, turning to Alice.

"A single bullet, but alas, no gun," Alice responded, her voice overwhelmed with melancholy.

"Pass it here," instructed the Dodo.

They congregated around her once more as the Dodo solemnly offered the bullet back to her, proclaiming, "We request you accept this refined ammunition;" and upon concluding this brief oration, they all erupted in spastic applause.

Alice found the entire episode ludicrous, yet the earnestness of the crowd dissuaded her from laughter. Afraid of triggering the mob, she simply curtsied and put the bullet back in her pocket, feigning appreciation. She was gripped in terror with the thought of the crowd turning on her and tearing her limb from limb.

The consumption of the "Doritos" ensued, breeding a cacophony of nauseating mouth sounds and streaks of orange powder clinging absurdly to the creatures. The larger birds bemoaned the tiny size of their snack, while the smaller ones struggled, choked, and in some cases, were saved only by the Dodo, who knew the Heimlich maneuver. Eventually, this tumult subsided into boredom, and they reassembled in a circle, eagerly soliciting the Sewer Rat for more of its narrative.

"You vowed to share your story," Alice reminded it, "and the reason for your aversion to—the 'C' word," she murmured surreptitiously, apprehensive of provoking the Sewer Rat's fight or flight instincts anew.

"I thought this was a safe space," the Sewer Rat replied indignantly. "Perhaps this poem by this year's Rodent Laureate award winner will help you check your privilege:"

There are some things
money can't buy
For everything else
there's Mastercard

"You're not even listening!" the Sewer Rat reprimanded Alice sternly. "Are you not subtly coerced to spend beyond your means?"

"I apologize," Alice responded, her voice meek with humility. "You are clearly the victim here."

"I am not!" exclaimed the Sewer Rat, sharply and with evident irritation.

"A knot?" questioned Alice, anxious to lighten the mood. "Oh, please let me help you untangle it!"

"I shall do nothing of the sort," retorted the Sewer Rat, rising and walking away. "You're a speciesist."

"I didn't mean any harm!" Alice implored, her voice tinged with regret. "But you are so easily offended!"

The Rat merely responded with a hiss.

"Please return and finish your story!" Alice called after it. The chorus of creatures echoed her plea, "Yes, please continue!" But the Sewer Rat only hastened its retreat, extending the middle finger of its paw back in Alice's direction.

"What a shame it wouldn't stay," lamented the Cockroach, as the Sewer Rat disappeared from view. Seizing the moment, an elderly Leech advised her daughter, "Speaking of MasterCard… It's important to build a good credit score and use debt to acquire assets that appreciate in value." To which the young Leech responded rather tersely, "Shut up bitch, I'm playing Fortnite."

"I do wish our Dienah were here," Alice proclaimed to no one in particular. "She'd catch that cursed mouse!"

"Dienah who?" inquired the Cockroach.

Alice grasped at the memory of her pet, feeling an eternity away from her past life.

"Dienah is – well, was – our cat. A remarkable slaughterer of rodents. She took no quarter. You wouldn't believe! And oh, if only you could have seen her chase and torture the birds! She would devour a mutant starling as easily as glance at it, taking her time to savor each bloody morsel… even the bones and eyeballs!"

Her words caused a notable stir among the assembled creatures. Several birds hastily flapped away: an old Magpie wrapped itself carefully, mumbling as it took flight, "The new season of 'Beheading Bachelors' is out." A morbidly obese Bald

Eagle, voice quivering, called to its offspring, "If you don't get in the fucking air right now I will pluck your feathers and stuff you back in your eggs." Under various pretenses, they all dispersed, leaving Alice in bleak solitude.

"If I ever want to get out of here," Alice reasoned, "I've got to stop talking about cats."

She shuddered at the thought of doing so. Would she forget Dienah altogether, leaving her a ghost of a memory never to be retrieved again?

The waterworks started up again as Alice, overcome by loneliness and despondency, began to weep anew. Snot poured down her face as her red eyes burned.

After a short while, her sobs were interrupted by the sound of something scurrying towards her, and she looked up with the tiniest spark of hope – either the Sewer Rat had reconsidered and was returning to read the rest of its "poem," or a predator was coming to end her misery and transfer the energy of her body into something that would at least be of use.

CHAPTER 4
RABBIT STEW

It was the Off-White Rabbit, staggering back, its demeanor fraught with anxiety, as though it had misplaced its heart medication. Alice overheard its frantic mutterings, "The Dutchmaster! The Dutchmaster! Oh, the plight of my paws! My fur and whiskers torn out! She'll taxidermize my head for this! Wherever could they have fallen?" Alice instantly surmised it was searching for its white kid gloves. She began to search as well, driven by a faint memory of what kindness was, but to no avail—the items had disappeared, along with the grand hall, the table, and the diminutive door, all incomprehensibly reconfigured by her dip in the cesspool.

Soon enough, the Rabbit spotted Alice rummaging around and, mistaking her for someone else, admonished her sharply, "Why, Mary Jane, what are you doing out here? Return home at once, and fetch me my gloves! Hurry, slave!" Overwhelmed by alarm and terrified of the consequences of defying this demand, Alice scurried away in the indicated direction, without attempting to rectify the Rabbit's error.

"He mistook me for hired help," Alice pondered as she hurried along. "What a shock it will be when he discovers my true identity! Yet, I should endeavor to retrieve his gloves—if they can be found. Perhaps then he will be indebted to help me escape this nightmare."

As she mulled this over, Alice stumbled upon a crumbling hovel, its door adorned with a dulled brass plate with the barely recognizable inscription "O. W. RABBIT." She silently entered without a knock, ascending the stairs swiftly, apprehensive about encountering the genuine Mary Jane and being hauled to prison for identity theft before locating the gloves.

"I have officially lost my mind," Alice mused to herself, "Home invasion. Running errands for a rabbit! Perhaps Dienah's reanimated corpse will start sending me on tasks next!" She let her imagination roam, envisioning such scenarios: "'Miss Alice! Come at once and shovel the turds from my litter box! Scoop up my warm vomit! Feed me at once or I will scratch you with claws caked in my own excrement!"

In a seemingly forgotten closet, she stumbled upon a table, barren save for a creepy collection of white kid gloves. Where did they come from, and were any children harmed in the process? She did not want to know the answer.

Grasping the gloves, she was poised to abandon this hollow sanctuary when her gaze was ensnared by a diminutive bottle, lurking near a mirror that reflected only despair. Void of any "DRINK ME" beckoning, she nonetheless uncorked its ominous contents and brought it to her withered lips. "Each morsel, each drop in this accursed realm heralds a twisted turn," she murmured, "Let's unveil the curse this potion holds. Perhaps it will restore my stature, for I am wearied of this insignificant form. If it's poison, then mercy is not far."

The transformation was swift and horrifying. Before half the acrid potion passed her lips, her head throbbed against the oppressive ceiling, forcing her to crouch, her neck screaming in protest. In panic, she abandoned the bottle, whispering to the shadows, "Enough of this madness—may I grow no more. Alas, escape is now a forlorn dream—I rue the moment I succumbed to this vile temptation!"

But her laments fell on deaf ears, swallowed by the relentless void. Her form, expanding uncontrollably, compelled her to kneel on the cold, unyielding floor. Moments later, even this meager refuge was usurped by her relentless growth, forcing her into a contorted sprawl, with one elbow jammed against the door and her arm twisted grotesquely around her head. Yet, her body continued its monstrous expansion, leaving her no choice but to thrust one arm outside, shattering the window, contorting a foot up the grimy chimney. "This is my limit, the end of my twisted journey," she whispered to the encroaching darkness. "Was I destined to die choking on soot, unable to move, slowly bleeding out?"

By some cruel twist of fate, the sinister potion ceased its torment, stabilizing her monstrous size. Trapped in this claustrophobic tomb, her massive form aching, the absence of hope was a tangible specter. With no conceivable escape from this existential prison, her despair deepened, a solitary soul ensnared in an endless labyrinth of misery.

In the gloom of her entrapment, Alice's thoughts drifted to her former life, a distant memory of mundane stability. "How quaint it was," she mused bitterly, "free from this relentless altering of form, not a pawn in the twisted games of rats and rabbits. I regret descending into this abyss. Yet, there's a perverse curiosity in this nightmare. I'm living a twisted fairy tale, far from the idyllic fantasies I once read. A tale of my misfortunes should be penned, a chronicle of despair. At least my suffering would not be in vain. But alas, I've outgrown my youth in this cramped tomb."

Then a new thought crept in, a dark solace. "Will I cease to age in this perpetual state? A morbid comfort, to be spared the decay of time. But an eternity without growth, forever shackled to ignorance. What a dreadful fate!"

Scolding herself, she whispered, "Foolish Alice, how can you entertain thoughts of surviving in this wretched place? There's scarcely room for your physical form, let alone your rapidly deteriorating mind."

Thus, she oscillated between despair and bitter contemplation, crafting a solitary dialogue in the gloom. But her reverie was interrupted by a voice from beyond her prison, a faint echo piercing her isolation. Eagerly, she ceased her internal debate and listened, desperate for any connection to the world outside her confinement.

"Mary Jane! Mary Jane!" the voice shrieked, a demand slicing through the oppressive silence. The sound of hurried shuffling echoed, a sinister harbinger. Alice knew it was the Rabbit, its haggard presence now an ominous sign in this forsaken world. Only pain had resulted from their interactions. She quivered, her colossal form causing the very foundations to shudder, momentarily forgetting her gargantuan size dwarfed the Rabbit's existence.

Soon, the Rabbit approached the door, its futile attempts to open it thwarted by Alice's massive elbow barricading it. The door, designed to swing inward, became an unyielding barrier. She heard the Rabbit mutter to itself about circumventing the entrance and breaking through another window.

"Have I not bled enough?", Alice wondered grimly. Lying in wait, she listened intently for the Rabbit's approach beneath the window. In a sudden, desperate move, she thrust out her hand, grasping at the void. She caught nothing but air, yet the sound of a shrill scream, a crash, and the shattering of glass filled the room. Alice surmised that the Rabbit might have met its grisly end, skewered through the heart by a fence post or some similar fate, a small victory in her endless night.

The air was soon pierced by the Rabbit's irate voice, "Osama! Osama! Where are you?" This was followed by a new, unfamiliar tone, "Are you blind? I'm digging for apples right here, you twit!"

"Digging for apples? Are you out of your skull?" the Rabbit retorted in fury. "Here! Come and assist me!" The sound of further glass destruction ensued, sharp debris scattering all about.

"Now, Osama, tell me, what's that monstrosity in the window?"

"What does it look like, whiskers? It's an arm, ya moron!"

"An arm, you fool! Who ever witnessed such a grotesque size? It's engulfing the entire window!"

"You blind?", the other voice screamed.

"Get this lumbering mass of flesh out of my house!"

the Rabbit commanded, its voice steeped in anger and disbelief. The surreal nature of the situation was not lost on Alice, who listened to this absurd exchange, a monstrous arm her only means of interacting with this bizarre and nightmarish world.

In the wake of the commotion, a heavy silence engulfed the room, punctuated only by intermittent whispers. Alice caught snippets of fearful reluctance, "Sure, I don't fancy it, ya scumbag, not one bit!" and the Rabbit's harsh retort, "Obey, you coward!" Seizing the moment, Alice stretched her hand out again, clawing at the void. This time, her action was met with dual shrieks and the familiar chorus of shattering glass. "Such an abundance of stupidity," Alice mused darkly. "What will they attempt now? If only they could extricate me from this nightmare. My eagerness to escape this purgatory knows no bounds."

Time passed in silent anticipation until at last, the rattle of cartwheels and a cacophony of voices reached her. Alice discerned the chaos of their conversation, a jumble of commands and protests about ladders, ropes, and the dubious sturdiness of the rotting roof. Amidst the uproar, a loud crash echoed, followed by accusations and a reluctant consensus that 'Epstein' the Sewer Rat was to descend the crumbling chimney.

"So, they consign Epstein to this grim task," Alice thought, a hint of dark amusement in her tone. "Poor

Epstein, burdened with their fears and tasks. I wouldn't trade places with him for all the tea in this forsaken land. This chimney may be narrow, but my foot can still find its mark."

Positioning her foot as far down the grimy chimney as possible, she listened intently for the telltale sounds of an unfortunate creature—Epstein, presumably—scrambling in the sooty confines above. Whispering to herself, "Here comes Epstein," she delivered a sharp kick, bracing herself for the unforeseen consequences of this desperate act of defiance in her surreal, oversized world.

The chaos outside crescendoed as Alice heard a chorus proclaim, "There goes Epstein!" followed by the Rabbit's commanding voice, "Catch him by the hedge!" Then, a haunting silence fell, soon shattered by a maelstrom of voices, a din of concern and confusion. "Support his head—Brandy, quickly—Don't let him suffocate—What befell you, old friend? Relate your ordeal!"

Then, a weak, tremulous voice pierced the air. Alice knew it to be Epstein's. "I... I can scarcely fathom it—No more, thank you; I've regained my senses. But I'm terribly concussed. All I recall is a force like an atom bomb propelling me skyward!"

"We thought you were dead for sure," the crowd responded.

Then, the Rabbit's voice cut through the air with a sinister decree, "We must incinerate the house! Burn it to the ground with everything inside! Build a Panera in its place!" To this, Alice bellowed with all her might, "Enough!"

An oppressive silence fell like a shroud. Alice pondered, "What will they concoct next? If they possessed any wit, they'd dismantle the roof." But she realized they were as dumb as they were mad. She heard the Rabbit plotting, "A barrowful will suffice for starters."

"A barrowful of what?" Alice wondered with a sense of foreboding. Her question was answered all too soon as stones came crashing through the window, slashing and bruising her face. Resolved to end this assault, she declared, "Stop or I'll pick up this house, drop it on you all, and affix your amputated feet to keychains for good luck!" Her command was met with another eerie silence, the world outside momentarily frozen by her defiance.

Alice, amidst the chaos, observed with a mix of astonishment and dread that the pebbles morphed into small Hostess gas station cupcakes upon hitting the ground. A glimmer of hope, or perhaps desperation, sparked within her. "If I consume one of these cupcakes," she pondered, "it must alter my size, or at least my DNA. Since I can hardly grow larger in this predicament, I shall inevitably shrink. And probably get cancer."

Though she had been repeatedly betrayed by similar rationalizations, her desperation knew no bounds and her faculties were rapidly escaping her. Bowel control was threatening to depart immediately.

With grim resolve, she ingested one of the unnaturally moist brown cakes, biting into a juicy maggot. Primal disgust quickly turned to a wave of anxiety as her body began to diminish. Once she had sufficiently shrunk, she darted out of the house, only to be greeted by a bizarre assembly of suffering animals and birds, among them the pitiful figure of Epstein the Sewer Rat, propped up by two diseased guinea pigs and being administered some malt liquor from a 40-ounce bottle. The crowd surged with vengeance towards Alice, so she fled into the presumed safety of a dense forest nearby.

Alone in the gloomy woods, Alice set her grim objectives: "First, regain my proper size. Second, find the entrance to that elusive garden. This seems a reasonable plan in a world unfit for reason."

The plan, simple in theory, was daunting in execution. Alice had no inkling of how to achieve these goals. As she wandered, her eyes searching the forest in vain, a sharp bark from above jolted her attention upwards, forcing her to confront yet another unforeseen and likely ominous encounter in this twisted, dark wonderland.

Hovering above her, a colossal, disheveled, visibly rabid stray dog peered down, its immense eyes round with curiosity, its massive paw outstretched in a feeble, albeit frightening attempt to touch her. Alice, mustering a tone of false cheer, tried to whistle to the creature, her heart pounding with the unsettling realization that its playful gesture could be a prelude to a more predatory interest.

Acting on instinct more than reason, Alice snatched up a fragment of stick, offering it to the gigantic hound. The dying creature, overcome with fear and anger, leapt towards the stick, its bark echoing with an unnerving rattle. It pretended to maul the stick, its massive form thrashing the wood to pieces. In a desperate bid for safety, Alice ducked behind a large Pfizer billboard, using it as a shield against the overwhelming creature. The orphan animal, undeterred, continued its frenzied pursuit, clumsily tumbling as it aimed for the sharp splinters flying through the air.

The game, akin to a dance of death with a beast of monumental proportions, left Alice fearing for her life. As she circled the mind-numbing advertisement, the dog alternated between ferocious charges and weary retreats, its hoarse barks filling the air. Finally, it collapsed, panting heavily, its massive tongue lolling out, eyes half-closed, wheezing in a death rattle.

Seizing this chance, Alice bolted, her feet pounding against the earth, her breath ragged with exertion. She ran until the thunderous barks faded into a distant echo, a haunting reminder of the fatal perils lurking in every corner of this oblivion.

Even amidst the terror, Alice couldn't help but reflect on the daunting creature she had just escaped. Leaning against a dead tree for support, she used a sheet of termite-chewed bark to fan the sweat on her brow, her mind a whirlwind of emotions. "Such an oddly endearing monstrosity" she mused with a tinge of irony. "If it had not been rabid, I would have enjoyed teaching it tricks, had I been of a size less likely to be devoured. Alas, I must focus on regaining my proper stature. But how? What must I consume to alter this predicament of ever-deepening insanity?"

Alice surveyed her surroundings — enormous wilted flowers, the towering blades of grass turning various shades of beige and brown — yet found nothing that seemed appropriate for her current needs. Her gaze then fell upon a large, rotting psilocybin mushroom, its stature rivaling her own. After a cursory inspection around its pungent base and sides, she decided to investigate its summit.

Balancing on tiptoes, Alice peered over the

mushroom's edge and was mortified to find herself gazing into the eyes of a colossal tapeworm. The creature twitched atop the mushroom, inhaling from a lengthy crack pipe with an air of total indifference to Alice's plight or the world itself. He exhaled acrid smoke that smelled of burning plastic.

CHAPTER 5
CRACKED-OUT TAPEWORM

In the midst of this persistently bizarre and disheartening world, Alice found herself locked in a silent stare with the bulging eyes of the Tapeworm, its spasmodic demeanor exuding an unhinged energy of exuberant violence. Finally, breaking the painfully awkward silence with a voice as cranked-up as its gaze, the Tapeworm spoke.

"Who the fuck are you?" it demanded, its tone devoid of warmth or welcome.

Alice, feeling diminutive and disoriented in the face of such a query, responded timidly, "Good question. I had a sense of who I was when today dawned, but now I struggle just to make sense of what's in front of my eyes, let alone what's behind them."

The Tapeworm's response was sharp and commanding. "Speak English, motherfucker!"

Alice, struggling to articulate the surreal and harrowing journey that had led her to this moment, felt the weight of her own confusion. Each transformation, each shift in size and perspective, had further estranged her from her own identity, leaving her adrift in a world where logic and constancy seemed as elusive as shadows in the eternal night.

Alice's attempt to explain her plight was met with the Tapeworm's indifferent and rude responses, further entrenching her sense of disorientation and isolation in this strange and unforgiving world.

"I can't explain myself, I'm afraid, sir," Alice confessed, her voice reflecting her internal turmoil, "because I'm not myself, you see."

The Tapeworm's reply was dismissive, "You ain't yourself cuz you ain't shit," showcasing its lack of empathy or understanding of Alice's existential crisis.

Frustrated yet polite, Alice tried to articulate the bewilderment of her changing form. "It's quite baffling to change sizes so frequently within a single day," she explained.

The Tapeworm, unimpressed, simply retorted, "The fuck you on about?"

Alice, striving to find common ground, pointed out the Tapeworm's impending metamorphosis into a chrysalis and then a butterfly, suggesting it might then understand her disconcertion. But the Tapeworm's indifferent "Whatchu know about being an insect?" response left her feeling more alienated.

Recognizing the futility of her explanation, Alice noted, "Perhaps your experience differs, but to me, it feels very strange."

The Tapeworm's scornful repetition of "Who the fuck are you?" looped the conversation back to its beginning, exacerbating Alice's frustration with its terse and unhelpful demeanor. She attempted to regain some control by insisting that the Tapeworm reveal its identity first, only to be met with a blunt "I ain't tellin' you shit."

Unable to formulate a response and wearied by the Tapeworm's obstinate mood, Alice turned to leave. However, the Tapeworm's call to return, promising something important, momentarily rekindled her hope for answers or guidance in this bewildering and dark landscape. Alice was lured back to the stinking mushroom, her curiosity piqued despite her growing exasperation.

"I'm five dollars short for the bus ticket back home!" the Tapeworm advised, its tone irritated and self-absorbed.

"Is that all?" Alice retorted, struggling to suppress her rising irritation.

"Nah," the Tapeworm responded, prolonging the enigmatic exchange.

Resigned to the possibility of gaining some insight, Alice decided to endure the Tapeworm's company. She watched as it frantically smoked its crack pipe, its awkward silence stretching on, staring off into space mumbling to itself. The vile insect noticed Alice and said, "Bitch, you crazy."

"I fear so, sir," Alice confessed, her voice heavy with melancholy. "My memory falters, and my size is in constant flux."

The Tapeworm, unfazed by her distress, simply instructed her to recite "This Is Why I'm Hot" by rap artist MIMS, steering their conversation into yet another bewildering direction. Alice, ensnared in this surreal and desensitizing world, found herself complying, her voice echoing the somber, haunting atmosphere that had come to define her existence.

This is why I'm hot
This is why I'm hot, yeah
This is why, This is why
This is why I'm hot, huh
This is why I'm hot
This is why I'm hot, ooh
This is why, this is why
This is why I'm hot

I'm hot 'coz I'm fly
You ain't 'coz you're not
This is why, this is why
This is why I'm hot
I'm hot 'coz I'm fly
You ain't 'coz you're not
This is why, this is why

This is why I'm hot

The whimsical and absurd words of the lyrics to "This Is Why I'm Hot," contrasted sharply with the bleak and distorted reality Alice was navigating. The playful absurdity of Shawn Maurice Mims's responses to the young woman's inquiries about his improbable attractiveness and the bizarre logic underpinning his explanations added a layer of dark humor to the grim atmosphere.

Each stanza, recounting Mims's outlandish abilities and his equally outlandish justifications, seemed to mirror Alice's own surreal experiences in this dark theater of absurdities. The final rebuke from Mims to the listener, threatening to shoot anyone who disrespects him, resonated with the harsh, unforgiving nature of the world Alice was trapped in.

As she finished her recitation, the absurdity of the poem stood in stark contrast to her predicament, highlighting the bizarre and often incomprehensible nature of her journey through a land where logic and reason were as elusive as the shifting shapes and sizes that continually haunted her existence.

The Tapeworm's blunt dismissal of Alice's recitation added to the oppressive atmosphere of confusion and frustration that enveloped her. Its declaration that her effort was "wack" further intensified the sense of disorientation and helplessness.

When the Tapeworm inquired about her preferred size, Alice, feeling small and insignificant, voiced her desire for a more substantial stature. "A bit larger, if you wouldn't mind, sir," she implored, "Three inches is a rather pitiful height."

The Tapeworm, taking umbrage at her words, asserted in an irate tone that three inches was normal and size didn't matter anyway, dramatically straightening itself to its full three inches in emphasis.

Alice, desperate and forlorn, attempted to explain her discomfort. "But I'm not accustomed to it," she said, her voice a blend of frustration and despair. Internally, she lamented the ease with which the creatures of this bizarre world took offense, adding to the sense of alienation and misunderstanding that plagued her journey.

The Tapeworm, dismissive of her plight, simply retorted that she would get used to it, before retreating back into the smoky haze of its crack pipe. Alice, left to grapple with the Tapeworm's indifferent advice, felt the weight of her solitary struggle.

Resigned to the unpredictable and surreal nature of her encounters, Alice waited with a patient, if weary, demeanor for the Tapeworm to resume its discourse. After a brief interlude marked by incoherent swearing and a brief seizure, the Tapeworm descended from its perch atop the mushroom and began to slither away into the dead grass. As it departed in a trail of putrid slime, it left behind a cryptic piece of guidance: "Rewind side A, fast-forward side B".

Alice, puzzled and intrigued, wondered silently, "Side A of what? Side B of what? Context!"

The Tapeworm, responding as though privy to her thoughts, clarified, "Of the fungus, fool." With these final words, it vanished from her sight, leaving Alice alone once again in the vast and bewildering expanse of this twisted world.

This enigmatic instruction about the mushroom presented both a glimmer of hope and a new quandary for Alice. The prospect of controlling her size was a tantalizing solution to one of her many predicaments. Yet, the ambiguity of the Tapeworm's advice, like so much in this strange land, offered no straightforward path, adding another layer to the onslaught of uncertainty and hardship that Alice had to navigate in what she desperately hoped was her journey back to some semblance of normalcy.

Confronted with the Tapeworm's disrespectful parting harassment, Alice scrutinized the mushroom, endeavoring to discern the sides to which it had cryptically referred. The mushroom's perfectly round shape presented an inscrutable puzzle. Nonetheless, she felt she had no choice but to once again throw caution to the wind, stretching her trembling arms around the mushroom and breaking off a piece from each side.

With a growing sense of uncertainty, Alice tentatively tasted a bit from the right-hand piece, only to experience an immediate and startling reaction. A sharp blow struck her underneath the chin, revealing that it was her own foot, a testament to the rapid shrinking caused by the piece she had just consumed. She reeled, teetering on the brink of unconsciousness.

Startled and alarmed by this abrupt transformation, Alice knew she had to act swiftly. She was diminishing at an alarming rate, leaving her no time for hesitation, lest she disappear entirely. The challenge of eating the other piece was exacerbated by her shrinking size, her chin now perilously close to her foot, constraining her ability to open her mouth. Despite these difficulties, she managed to consume a morsel of the left-hand piece of the mushroom, hoping to counteract the disconcerting effects of her rapid diminution and regain some control over her fluctuating size.

Alice's initial relief switched to alarm as she discovered a new, sanity-stealing predicament. Looking down, she saw no trace of her shoulders, only a lengthy expanse of beck studded with bulging veins, stretching down like a stalk into the overgrown, abyssal canopy below.

Puzzled and concerned, she questioned aloud, "What are all these invasive plant species? Where have my shoulders vanished to? And my poor hands, why can't I see you?" Despite her attempts to locate her hands by moving them, the only response was a slight rustling in the distant wilted foliage.

Realizing the futility of bringing her hands to her head, Alice endeavored to lower her head to them instead. To her astonishment and horror, she found her neck to be surprisingly flexible, bending with serpentine ease. She awkwardly maneuvered it into a zigzag, preparing to delve into the dying leaves below, which she now recognized as the treetops she had been traversing earlier. Her esophagus contorted painfully. Breathing became difficult.

Her traumatic transformation was abruptly interrupted by a startling encounter. A dirt-covered pigeon swooped at her, its wings flapping aggressively, striking her face. The pigeon's sudden and violent appearance forced Alice to swiftly contort her elongated neck, pulling back from the unexpected and hostile confrontation.

The Pigeon's eyes bulged, oozing pus. "Serpent!", it shrieked. Alice's frightening bewilderment turned the meager contents of her stomach. She vehemently denied being a serpent, but her protestations, as usual, seemed to be entirely ignored. The Pigeon, excreting a stream of white waste as it dove, continued its assault while ignoring Alice's impotent attempt at clarification.

Consumed by its own troubles, the sickly bird recounted its unsuccessful efforts to protect its eggs from poisonous serpents, wondering aloud if the exercise was ultimately futile. Alice could relate. Its tirade about the challenges of egg-hatching and the incessant threat of serpents revealed deep-seated fear and post-traumatic stress which she was all too familiar with at this point.

Startled by a pang of sympathy, Alice offered her apologies for the Pigeon's troubles, despite her own bewildered state. The Pigeon, however, remained fixated on its plight, lamenting its choice of a high tree for safety, only to encounter what it perceived as a serpent descending from the sky to murder its babies.

Alice, still trying to assert her identity, was interrupted by the Pigeon's demanding query, "Well! What are you?" The bird's accusation that she was fabricating her identity added another layer of surreal frustration to Alice's exceedingly disorienting journey.

Alice's insistence that she was a little girl was met with scornful disbelief from the Pigeon, who pointed out there was obviously nothing little about her. The Pigeon's cognitive dissonance was unassailable. In its puny brain, Alice was a serpent, a harbinger of death.

Attempting to defend herself, Alice admitted to having eaten eggs in the past, but pointed out that this was common behavior for little girls, not just serpents. This infuriated the Pigeon, which screamed indecipherable epithets, hateful spittle pouring from its cracked beak. Alice was stunned into silence.

Seizing upon Alice's dumbfoundedness, the Pigeon accused her of being an egg fiend, indifferent to whether she was a girl or a serpent. Alice, growing increasingly exasperated with the absurd accusations, clarified that she was not constantly seeking eggs and, even if she were, she had no interest in the Pigeon's eggs, particularly raw ones.

"Oh, my eggs aren't good enough for you?," the Pigeon said dismissively, finally disappearing in a frenzied flap of feathers. Shaken by the encounter, Alice navigated her way through the trees, her unnaturally elongated neck complicating her progress as it entwined with the branches, requiring frequent pauses to untangle herself. She feared she would tie her own neck in a knot and die of asphyxiation. Amidst this struggle, she recalled the rotting mushroom pieces still in her possession, the key to adjusting her size.

With deliberate care, Alice alternated between nibbling on each piece of mushroom, experiencing fluctuating heights and the associated pain of her internal organs, skeletal structure and nervous system contorting in wildly unnatural, inhuman dimensions. Her efforts were eventually rewarded as she regained her normal stature. This return to a familiar size, after enduring such a series of tortuous transformations, now felt ironically unfamiliar.

Her attention quickly shifted to the next part of her plan — accessing the elusive garden. While pondering her next move, she stumbled upon a small homeless encampment that appeared to house Smurfs or some other kind of diminutive race. Tarps were slung low to the ground, and discarded cardboard boxes labeled with illustrations of smiles and the word "Amazon" were lined up on a slab of cracked concrete that mysteriously emerged from the forest floor.

Concerned about the reaction her current size might provoke from the locals, Alice decided to reduce her stature further. She cautiously nibbled on the right-hand piece of mushroom, carefully modulating her size until she was a mere nine inches tall. Only then did she feel remotely comfortable approaching the sprawling and dilapidated campground, afraid she would be set upon by frenzied junkies but mildly hopeful she'd find someone to help her.

CHAPTER 6
PIG ROAST

For several awkward moments, she lingered, gazing at the dilapidated homeless camp, pondering her next move in this desolate world. Abruptly, a bearded acid casualty clad in Birkenstocks and a tattered Grateful Dead hoodie emerged from the terrifyingly dark forest—(she surmised he was an acid casualty due to his garb: otherwise, his grimy visage would have led her to believe he was more ferret than man)—and hammered violently at the door with bony knuckles. The portal was answered by another Deadhead, his attire equally ragged, sporting a bulbous face, and eyes reminiscent of a frog's unblinking stare; both, Alice observed, bore hair dusted with the ash of a world gone to ruin, curling wildly about their heads. Her curiosity piqued, she edged closer to eavesdrop, concealed by the sound of far-off animals screaming in agony.

The Ferret commenced by extracting from behind his back a rusty nitrous tank, almost as large as himself, and dragged it to his counterpart, uttering in a grave tone, "Hit this." The Frog did as he was told, exhaled deeply, in an equally grave tone, said, "Bro."

Then, they both nodded deeply, on the edge of

losing consciousness, their ashen curls intertwining in a grotesque dance. They finally passed out in a heap on top of one another.

Alice's laughter, a rare and hollow sound in this bleak world, forced her to retreat deeper into the sinister woods, lest she be overheard. When she dared to look again, the Ferret had disappeared, and the other sat on the charred earth near the door, gazing vacantly upwards into the gray, lifeless sky, tears streaming down his face. Down the path she spied a decrepit flophouse.

Alice approached the door with trepidation and knocked, her heart echoing trembling with each tap.

"Cops are back," declared the Junkie, his voice a hollow echo. Within, there was an unending cacophony—a relentless wailing and screaming, punctuated by thunderous crashes, as if porcelain and metal were shattering into deadly shrapnel.

"Please," implored Alice, "how may I enter this forsaken place?"

"Nobody's home, man," the Junkie droned, oblivious to her plea, "you got a cigarette?" His gaze never left the bleak sky above, a gesture Alice found deeply discourteous. "Perhaps he cannot control it," she mused silently, "his eyes are almost swallowed by his skull. Yet, he could at least respond to my query.—

How do I enter?" she asked again, louder.

"Bro said he'd be here by now," intoned the Junkie, as if to the void.

In that instant, the house's door swung open, and a large Ronald Reagan 40th President commemorative plate hurtled out, narrowly missing the Junkie's head. It shattered against a tree behind him, with fragments of shrapnel flying everywhere.

"—are you holding?" the Junkie droned on, his tone unaltered, as if the near-miss and destruction were but everyday occurrences.

"How can I possibly enter?" Alice inquired once more, her voice rising with desperation.

"We can fix you up," retorted the Junkie, "if you got something to share."

Alice found no comfort in the offer. "This is truly horrific," she murmured to herself, "the way all these addicts can think of only one thing!" Her words were a hoarse gasp against the backdrop of a world gone mad.

The Junkie, seizing the moment, repeated his words with a dismal variation. "I got a kit," he intoned, "if you got the fix."

"What do you expect me to do?" Alice implored. "Whatever," replied the Junkie, commencing a hollow whistle.

"Oh, conversing with him is futile," Alice declared in despair: "He's utterly senseless!" With that, she screamed, "Police! Stop resisting!", kicked the door down and stepped inside.

The door opened directly into a grease-stained kitchen, choked with smoke from end to end: the Dutchmaster was perched on a rickety three-legged stool, cradling a wailing infant; the cook, hunched over the fire, stirred a large cauldron that seemed to bubble with a murky soup that caused the home to smell of burning garbage.

"Is that soup or methamphetamines?", Alice thought to herself, coughing and sneezing amidst the pungent air.

The house was indeed saturated with noxious meth fumes. Even the Dutchmaster succumbed to the occasional sneeze; the baby, however, was caught in an endless cycle of sneezing and wailing, a symphony of mucus and discomfort. The only beings in the kitchen immune to the chemical onslaught were the cook and a large mangy cat, lounging on the hearth, its grin stretching unnaturally wide, mouth covered in blood.

"Please, could you inform me," Alice ventured, her voice hesitant as she was uncertain of the propriety of speaking first, "why your cat grins in such a manner?"

"It's a Gutter cat," the Dutchmaster responded, "and that's the reason. Swine!"

The last word was uttered with such abrupt ferocity that Alice flinched; however, she quickly realized it was aimed at the baby, not her. Emboldened, she continued:—

"I was unaware that Gutter cats always grinned; in truth, I never imagined that cats could grin at all."

"All of them can," the Dutchmaster declared; "and most of them indeed do grin."

"I've never known any that do," Alice replied tentatively.

"You know very little," the Dutchmaster retorted sharply; "dumbass."

Alice found the tone of this comment quite disagreeable and thought it prudent to steer the conversation towards another topic. As she searched for a new subject, the cook, in a sudden frenzy, removed the cauldron from the fire and began hurling everything within her grasp at the

Dutchmaster and the wailing infant—the first missiles were chemistry beakers, quickly followed by a barrage of glass pipes, syringes, surgical tubing and burnt spoons. The Dutchmaster seemed utterly indifferent to the assault, even when struck; the baby, already in a state of constant howling, showed no discernible reaction to the impact of the flying objects. It almost looked excited. She could see white and black paint on the child's face and a gold chain from which dangled a 14-karat gold-clad pendant of a crazy clown running with a butcher's knife. It was a juggalo baby.

"Whoop whoop!" Alice exclaimed, her voice a mix of panic and distress. "You almost scalped that baby with the cookware," she cried out as a particularly large Pyrex casserole dish whizzed perilously close.

"If everyone minded their own business," the Dutchmaster growled hoarsely, "the world would spin much faster than it currently does."

"And kill everyone in the process?" Alice questioned passionately, seizing the chance to demonstrate her knowledge. "Consider the turmoil it would cause with day and night! The earth, you see, takes twenty-four hours to complete a rotation on its axis—"

"Speaking of axes," the Dutchmaster interrupted, "dismember this waste of flesh!"

Alice cast a worried glance at the cook, wondering if she would act upon this ominous suggestion. However, the cook was deeply engrossed in stirring the meth, appearing oblivious to the conversation. Alice continued, albeit with uncertainty: "Twenty-four hours, I believe; or is it twelve? I—"

"Fake news," the Dutchmaster snapped; "Numbers aren't real!" Resuming her rough handling of the juggalo child, she rapped a disturbing bar, punctuating each line with a violent jerk:

I fed a fish to a pelican at 'Frisco bay
It tried to eat my cell phone, he ran away
And music is magic, pure and clean
You can feel it and hear it, but it can't be seen

The baby juggalo joined in:

"Whoop whoop!"

As the Dutchmaster belted out the second verse, she continued to hurl the infant up and down with alarming ferocity. The infant's cries were so piercing that Alice struggled to make out the lyrics:

Water, fire, air, and dirt
Fucking magnets, how do they work?
And I don't wanna talk to a scientist
Y'all motherfuckers lying, and getting me pissed

"Whoop whoop!"
"Mandatory adoption!" the Dutchmaster barked at Alice, tossing the infant her way as she spoke. "I must prepare for croquet with the Queen of Heart Emojis," and with that, she hastened from the room. The cook, in a gesture of defiance, hurled broken glass tubing in her wake, grazing her skull and leaving a blood-spurting gash.

Catching the baby juggalo proved a challenge for Alice, as it was grotesquely misshapen, its limbs stretching out in every direction, "resembling an obese goth starfish dying on the beach," Alice thought. The infant juggalo sputtered and puffed like a broken vape pen upon being caught, continuously contorting and then stretching itself out, making it quite a task for Alice to simply maintain her hold without dropping it on the head for at least the second time in its life. It vomited a little onto her hair, but Alice was too distracted to notice.

Once she discerned the peculiar manner of caring for the infant, which involved twisting it into a knot-like shape and firmly holding its right ear and left foot to prevent it from unraveling, Alice decided to take it outside. "If I don't remove this juggalo child from here," Alice pondered, "they will surely end its life within a day or two: would it not be akin to murder to abandon it?" She voiced these thoughts aloud, and the small creature grunted in response, having ceased its sneezing by then. "Do not grunt," Alice admonished; "it's unbecoming, even of a juggalo." The baby grunted once more, prompting Alice to scrutinize its features with concern. Undeniably, it had a very upturned nose, resembling a snout more than a typical nose; moreover, its eyes appeared unusually small for an infant. Alice found the appearance of the creature unsettling. "Yet, it might merely be emo," she reasoned and peered into its eyes again, searching for tears.

No tears were present. "If you are destined to become a pig," Alice spoke earnestly, "then you will be a free range, organic one." The small creature emitted another sound, a mix of a sob and a grunt, leaving Alice in doubt as to its nature. They continued in awkward silence for some time.

Alice had just begun to wonder, "What shall I do with this juggalo once I return home?" when it let out a particularly forceful grunt, causing her to glance down at it in alarm. This time, the truth was unmistakable: it was a pig, and she felt absurd at the thought of carrying it any longer. If anything, she thought, she should slaughter it and enjoy a bacon sandwich.

She placed the pig on the ground, feeling a sense of relief as it trotted away into the forest. "Had it grown up," she mused, "it would have been a most unsightly child, but as a pig, it is rather handsome." Her thoughts wandered to other children she knew who might be better off as pigs, and she was pondering, "If only one knew the proper method to transform them—" when she was startled to feel a warm, wet trickle on her shoulder. The Gutter Cat was pissing on her from a tree branch above.

The Gutter Cat only grinned when Alice looked up with a nauseous grimace. It seemed amiable, she thought, but its long claws and numerous teeth reminded her to maintain a respectful distance.

"Cat piss," she began tentatively, unsure if the Gutter Cat had seen her; however, it responded by grinning even wider. "Well, it seems to be content with that," Alice thought, and continued. "Could you stop urinating on me and advise me on which direction I should take from here?"

"That largely depends on your desired destination," the Gutter Cat replied, mercifully redirecting its stream.

"I don't particularly care where—" Alice began.

"Then it's irrelevant which path you choose," the Gutter Cat interjected.

"—just so long as I end up somewhere," Alice added by way of clarification.

"You're certain to accomplish that," the Gutter Cat

assured her, "if you simply walk long enough." Alice conceded the truth in this, so she attempted a different question. "Is this neighborhood safe?"

"In that direction," the Gutter Cat gestured with its right paw, "lives a total Hater: and in that direction," indicating with the other paw, "resides a bloodthirsty Mosquito. Choose whichever you prefer: they're both insane."

"I'd rather not encounter insane people," Alice remarked.

"That's unavoidable here," the Gutter Cat declared: "we're all insane. I'm insane. You're insane."

"How can you be sure I'm insane?" Alice queried.

"You must be," the Gutter Cat reasoned, "otherwise you wouldn't have arrived here."

Alice did not find this to be a convincing argument; nonetheless, she persisted, "And how can you be certain of your own insanity?"

"To start with," the Gutter Cat began, "a dog isn't mad. You'll agree with that, right?"

"I suppose so," Alice conceded.

"Well, then," the Gutter Cat continued, "consider this:

a dog growls when it's angry and wags its tail when it's pleased. Now, I growl when I'm pleased and wag my tail when I'm angry. Hence, I am mad."

"I'd say that's more purring than growling," Alice remarked.

"Name it as you will," the Gutter Cat replied. "Will you be playing croquet with the Queen of Heart Emojis today?"

"Who? I mean… I'd be very keen to," Alice responded, "but I haven't received an invitation as of yet."

"You'll encounter me there," the Gutter Cat stated, and then it disappeared into thin air.

Alice, now accustomed to the bizarre occurrences in this world, was hardly startled by the Gutter Cat's sudden reappearance.

"By the way," inquired the Gutter Cat, "what happened to the baby juggalo? I almost forgot to ask."

"It transformed into a pig," Alice replied nonchalantly, as if such an event was entirely ordinary.

"Whoop whoop," remarked the Gutter Cat, before

vanishing once more into the ether.

Alice lingered briefly, half-expecting the Gutter Cat to reappear, but it did not. After a few moments, she continued on her path towards the Mosquito's abode. "I've encountered plenty of haters before," she mused; "the Mosquito will likely be far more intriguing, and perhaps, since it's nuclear winter, it won't be as wild for my blood as it might have been in summer." As she pondered this, she looked up and, to her surprise, saw the Gutter Cat perched on a tree branch once again.

"Did you say pig, or cig?" the Gutter Cat queried.

"I said pig," Alice responded; "and I do wish you would stop appearing and disappearing so abruptly: it's quite disorienting."

"Very well," agreed the Gutter Cat; and this time, it stuck its middle finger out as it disappeared gradually, starting with the tip of its tail and ending with its blood-soaked grin, which eerily remained for a while after the rest of it had vanished.

"Well! I've often seen a cat without a grin," Alice thought to herself, "but a grin without a cat! What the hell is that?"

Not long after her encounter with the Gutter Cat, Alice came within view of the Mosquito's dwelling. It seemed unmistakably correct, given its chimney was sculpted into the shape of a proboscis and the roof was thatched with what appeared to be used Band-Aids. The house's size was intimidating, prompting Alice to hesitate. She decided to nibble some more of the mushroom she had kept from earlier, adjusting her size to about two feet tall before approaching. Even then, she neared the house with trepidation, thinking to herself, "What if it is utterly mad? I'm starting to wish I had chosen to visit the Hater instead!"

CHAPTER 7
MOCHA FRAPPUCINO

Beneath a gnarled, lifeless tree, in the fallow courtyard of a crumbling psychiatric hospital, sat a cafeteria table. It appeared to have been thrown out of the shattered window above. Here, the Mosquito and the Hater, ghastly specters of a bygone era, partook in a macabre wine mixer. A Slug, caught in an eternal slumber, lay between them, denigrated to the role of footrest. They dug their heels into its inert form, conversing in menacing tones. Alice, observing this grotesque scene, mused silently, "A cruel fate for the Slug, but in its endless sleep, perhaps ignorance is its bliss."

The table, though vast and sprawling, hosted this grim assembly in just one corner. As Alice approached, the air filled with cries of "No room! No room!", a chorus of despair echoing in the desolate landscape. Defiant, Alice declared, "There's more than enough room in this desolate wasteland," and settled into an oversized, decrepit armchair, its fabric as worn as the world around her.

"Partake in our intoxicating vintage," coaxed the Mosquito, his voice a mixture of temptation and doom.

Alice's gaze swept across the table, a barren

landscape save for copious amounts of expensive-looking glasses and dishware. "I see no wine here," she observed, her voice echoing in the desolate space.

"Indeed, there is none," replied the Mosquito, his words as empty as the world they inhabited.

"Then it was a hollow jest to offer it," retorted Alice, her anger flaring like a lone spark in a void of despair.

"Just as hollow as your intrusion at this table without an invitation," countered the Mosquito, his tone sharp like the edge of the world.

"I was unaware it belonged to anyone," Alice defended, "especially when it's set for far more than three lost souls."

"Let's circle back to that later. Your hair wants cutting," interjected the Hater abruptly, his eyes having studied Alice with a curiosity born of madness. This strange proclamation marked his first foray into their bleak exchange.

"Personal remarks are the refuge of the thoughtless," Alice chided, her voice carrying a weight of solemnity; "such rudeness is unbecoming."

The Hater's eyes widened, orbs reflecting a world gone mad, yet his response was cryptic as ever: "Why is a Dodo like humanity?"

Alice's mind, weary from the desolation around her, found a spark of interest. "Ah, a riddle amidst ruin," she mused internally. Aloud, she professed, "I believe I might unravel this enigma."

"Do you claim to fathom its depths?" inquired the Mosquito, his voice echoing like a hollow wind.

"Precisely," affirmed Alice.

"Then speak your thoughts plainly," continued the Mosquito.

"I endeavor to do so," Alice responded quickly; "what I say is what I mean."

"Incoherent!" the Hater interjected sharply. "To declare 'I see what I eat' equates to 'I eat what I see' – akin to embracing madness and diabetes!"

"And to say," added the Mosquito, "that 'I cherish what I receive' is the same as 'I receive what I cherish' is to ignore the cruel whims of fate!"

"And you might as well claim," murmured the Slug, surprising Alice, who had assumed it was dead, "that 'I breathe in slumber' is identical to 'I slumber in breath!'"

"In your case," concluded the Hater, his voice a final note in their macabre symphony, "it is all one and the same." The conversation then fell into silence, a void as profound as the mysteries of Dodos and humanity, of which Alice knew preciously little.

The silence, thick as the fog of desolation, was shattered by the Hater's abrupt inquiry. "Are you late or early? What day were you supposed to be here? Did I miss the Zoom call?" he asked, turning to Alice with a sense of urgency. He clutched a watch, its gears choked by time and neglect, shaking it sporadically, holding it close to his ear as if expecting it to whisper secrets lost to the ages.

Alice, her mind adrift in the sea of absurdity, guessed, "What day is it, even?"

"Two days astray," lamented the Hater with a sigh that seemed to carry the weight of eons. "I warned that Venti, quad-shot, non-fat, extra-hot, no-foam, with whip, double-blended, caramel drizzle, chocolate chip, mocha frappuccino with a half-pump of peppermint, a quarter-pump of vanilla, a half-pump of cinnamon, a splash of soy milk, a sprinkle of matcha powder, a dash of nutmeg, light ice, and topped with pumpkin spice topping was ill-suited for its mechanisms!" His gaze, filled with a tempest of irritation, fell upon the Mosquito.

"It was the finest Venti, quad-shot, non-fat, extra-hot,

no-foam, with whip, double-blended, caramel drizzle, chocolate chip, mocha frappuccino with a half-pump of peppermint, a quarter-pump of vanilla, a half-pump of cinnamon, a splash of soy milk, a sprinkle of matcha powder, a dash of nutmeg, light ice, and topped with pumpkin spice topping in these desolate times," the Mosquito retorted softly, almost apologetically.

"Rot from the ruins of civilization must have infiltrated," grumbled the Hater, his voice a low rumble of discontent. "You should have spared it the contamination of the unwashed Starbucks bathroom."

The Mosquito, carefully cradling the watch as one might pick up a cursed relic, peered into its shattered face with a gloom that mirrored the world around them. He submerged it in his empty wine glass, as if hoping the imaginary liquid might cleanse it of its temporal ailments, but upon inspecting it again, found no words to express his dismay, save for the melancholic repetition, "It was indeed the best Venti, quad-shot, non-fat, extra-hot, no-foam, with whip, double-blended, caramel drizzle, chocolate chip, mocha frappuccino with a half-pump of peppermint, a quarter-pump of vanilla, a half-pump of cinnamon, a splash of soy milk, a sprinkle of matcha powder, a dash of nutmeg, light ice, and topped with pumpkin spice topping in this forsaken world."

Alice peered over the shadowed figure's shoulder, her eyes tracing the bizarre and broken contraption. "What an odd timepiece!" she observed, her voice tinged with a mix of fear and fascination. "It marks the days in this endless cycle, yet fails to reveal the hour in this timeless hellscape!"

"And why should it?" the Hater rasped, his voice a hoarse whisper in the desolate air. "Does your relic of a watch disclose the year in this unending apocalypse?"

"Certainly not," Alice retorted, her voice hollow, echoing the desolation around them: "But that's because the years blend into a singular, unending nightmare."

"A sentiment shared by my own timepiece," the Hater declared with a hollow laugh.

Confusion and dread swirled within Alice. The Hater's words were a cryptic puzzle, a mad riddle in the language of despair. "Your words are a dark labyrinth I cannot navigate," she admitted, her politeness fraying at the edges.

"The Slug succumbs again to the slumber of oblivion," the Hater noted, dousing its swollen nose with an unidentified curdled liquid.

The Slug, trapped in its eternal daze, murmured

without opening its eyes, "Indeed, indeed; the very thought I was about to voice in this absurd theater of the damned."

"Have you unraveled the enigma?" the Hater asked, his gaze returning to Alice's haunted eyes.

"I surrender," Alice replied, her voice a whisper in the desolate wind: "What is the solution?"

"I am as lost as you," confessed the Hater.

"Likewise," murmured the Mosquito.

Alice exhaled a sigh that seemed to carry the weight of the world. "Perhaps our time might be better spent more wisely," she said, "than squandered on unsolvable mysteries."

"If you were intimate with Time as I am," the Hater spoke with a bitter edge, "you wouldn't speak of squandering it. Time is a living specter."

"I can't grasp your meaning," Alice admitted.

"Of course, you can't!" the Hater sneered. "I wager you've never even whispered to Time in the void!"

"Maybe not," Alice responded cautiously: "But I have battled against time in my attempts to survive a forgotten world."

"Aha! That explains it," the Hater exclaimed. "Time detests being challenged. If you were in harmony with him, he might twist the clock to your whims. Imagine, if it were nine in the morning, the time to commence lessons: a mere suggestion to Time, and the clock would spin wildly! Half-past one, a mirage of lunch time!"

("I wish it were so," the Mosquito whispered to itself.)

"That would be a wonder," Alice mused, "but then — I doubt my hunger would align with such illusion."

"Maybe not initially," the Hater said: "But you could trap time at half-past one for eternity if you wished."

"Is that your method of command?" Alice inquired, her voice echoing the desolation around them.

The Hater's head drooped in sorrow. "Not I," he lamented. "We fell into discord last March — just as he plunged into madness," he said, nodding grimly towards the Mosquito. "It was during the nightmarish symphony of the Queen of Heart Emojis, where I was compelled to perform:

'Tinkle, tinkle, sewer rat!
Came to pee, instead you shat!'

You might be familiar with this lament?"

"I've encountered a semblance of it," Alice replied.

"It continues, you know," the Hater droned on, "in this manner:

*Far inside the depths of hell,
Like a secret none will tell.
tinkle, tinkle —* '"

At this, the Slug stirred, murmuring in its haunted sleep "tinkle, tinkle, tinkle, tinkle —" its voice a haunting echo that forced them to silence it.

"I had scarcely begun the initial verse," the Hater recounted, "when the Queen erupted in fury, shrieking, 'Epic fail! Off with his head!'"

"How terribly barbaric!" Alice exclaimed.

"And from that moment," the Hater continued in a tone laden with sorrow, "Time defies my every request! Eternally, it remains six o'clock."

An insight flickered in Alice's mind, like a lone candle in an endless night. "Is that why this tableau of upscale, handcrafted, artisanal, fair-trade tableware is perpetually laid out?" she questioned.

"Yes, that's the grim reality," the Hater responded with a weary exhale: "It's eternally an upper-middle-class biodynamic wine mixer in this forsaken loop, and there's no respite to cleanse the remnants of our despair."

"So, you continually drift in a futile circle?" Alice deduced.

"Precisely," confirmed the Hater: "as we deplete the instruments of our endless mingling."

"And what fate awaits when you return to where this cycle began?" Alice dared to inquire.

"Let's abandon this dreary topic," the Mosquito interjected, stifling a yawn. "I grow weary of it. Entertain us, ugly human."

"I fear I know not how," Alice admitted, her voice quivering at the suggestion.

"Then let the Slug be our storyteller!" they both demanded. "Awaken, Slug!" And they pinched it simultaneously from both sides.

The Slug lethargically opened his eyes. "I wasn't lost in slumber," he croaked weakly: "I have been a silent and reluctant witness to your bleak discourse."

"Share with us a tale!" implored the Mosquito.

"Yes, please," Alice echoed, her plea tinged with

abject desperation.

"And be swift," the Hater added sharply, "lest you succumb to the claws of sleep before your story reaches its end."

"In an age long past, there were three quadriplegic sisters," the Slug began hastily; "named Karen, Kim, and Taylor; condemned to dwell at the abyssal bottom of a well—"

"What sustained them?" Alice interjected, her mind always wandering to matters of sustenance in this desolate world.

"They subsisted on Mountain Dew," the Slug replied after a moment's contemplation.

"That couldn't be," Alice remarked softly; "such a diet would surely be their doom."

"And doomed they were," the Slug confirmed; "gravely so."

Alice endeavored to envision this bizarre existence, but the concept was too alien, too distorted. So she pressed on: "But what led them to inhabit the depths of a well?"

"Indulge in more wine," the Mosquito suggested to Alice, with a grave intensity.

"I've yet to partake in any," Alice responded, her tone laced with indignation, "thus I cannot partake in more."

"You imply you can't have less," the Hater interjected: "it's far simpler to exceed nothing."

"Your input wasn't sought," Alice retorted.

"Who now delves into personal affronts?" the Hater declared, a hollow triumph in his voice.

Alice, lost in the maddening depths of this absurd conversation, silently served herself some imaginary wine and moldy bread-and-butter, then turned back to the Slug, reiterating her inquiry. "Why did they reside at the well's abyss?"

The Slug again paused to contemplate before replying, "It was a well of delicious Mountain Dew."

"There's no such thing!" Alice began, her voice rising in frustration, but she was swiftly silenced by the hushed tones of the Hater and the Mosquito, and the Slug, now irate, retorted, "If civility eludes you, perhaps you should narrate the tale yourself."

"No, please continue," Alice implored with newfound humility; "I'll hold my peace. Perhaps such a place does exist."

"Perhaps indeed!" the Slug scoffed. Yet, he agreed to proceed. "Thus, these three forsaken sisters—they were endeavoring to learn consumer packaged goods production, you understand—"

"What were they creating?" Alice interjected, momentarily forgetting her vow of silence.

"Mountain Dew," the Slug replied, not pausing to reflect this time.

"I desire a fresh cup," the Hater interjected abruptly: "Let us all shift one seat over."

As he spoke, the Hater shifted his position, and the Slug trailed after him. The Mosquito then occupied the Slug's former spot, leaving Alice, somewhat reluctantly, to take the Mosquito's blood-stained seat. The Hater seemed to benefit from this change, whereas Alice found her situation worsened, particularly as the Mosquito had just spilled a bucket of pus into his plate.

Eager not to upset the Slug again, Alice proceeded with caution: "But I'm puzzled. How did they extract the Mountain Dew?"

"One draws water from a water-well," the Hater explained; "thus, it stands to reason one could draw Mountain Dew from a Mountain Dew well—doesn't it, dimwit?"

"But they were inside the well," Alice pointed out to the Slug, deliberately ignoring the Hater's last jab.

"Precisely," the Slug affirmed; "deep within."

This response only added to Alice's confusion, causing her to let the Slug continue without further interruption.

"They were learning the art of logo design," the Slug continued, its voice weary, its eyes heavy with drowsiness; "and they drew all things imaginable — everything beginning with an 'M' —"

"Why an 'M'?" Alice inquired.

"Why not?" retorted the Mosquito.

Alice lapsed into silence, her mind a whirlpool of unanswered questions and surreal absurdities.

By this point, the Slug had surrendered to slumber, its eyes sealed shut, drifting into a fitful doze. However, a sharp pinch from the Hater jolted it awake with a startled yelp, and it resumed: " — beginning with 'M', such as mouse-traps amidst ruins, the mournful moon, melancholic memories, and the madness of muchness — you've heard the phrase 'much of a muchness' — but have you ever beheld a depiction of such madness?"

Alice, utterly befuddled, responded, "Truly, now that you question it, I cannot conceive—"

"Then silence should be your companion," the Hater interrupted sharply.

This brusque remark was the final straw for Alice. She rose in a wave of indignation and strode away; the Slug instantly succumbed again to sleep, and neither the Hater nor the Mosquito acknowledged her departure, though she glanced back several times, half-desiring them to beckon her return. The last glimpse she had of them was their attempt to stuff the Slug into the salt shaker.

"I shall never venture there again!" Alice declared as she navigated the barren woods. "This has been the most ludicrous and dismal happy hour in my existence, and I've been to Applebee's!"

As she made this proclamation, she observed a tree with a door embedded within its trunk. "How peculiar," she mused. "But then, today abounds in peculiarities. Perhaps it's best to just enter and hope for the best." And with that, she stepped through the cobwebbed doorway.

Alice emerged once again into the elongated hall, its walls whispering of forgotten tales, standing near the diminutive table. "This time, I shall navigate this haunted maze with more wisdom," she murmured to herself. She commenced her endeavor by seizing the tarnished golden key, unlocking the portal that led to the overgrown garden, a glimpse of what lay beyond filled with both allure and foreboding.

With deliberate care, she nibbled on the fragment of rotting mushroom she had preserved in her pocket, each bite an act of transformation. Gradually, she diminished to a mere foot in height, her organs once again contracting in intense discomfort, like the morning after eating a late-night Domino's pizza. Navigating the narrow corridor, a sense of anticipation and unease intertwining within her, she finally found herself stepping into the dense, stinking undergrowth.

It was a surreal landscape, starkly contrasting with the bleakness she had traversed. Wilting beds of flowers glowed like irradiated fuel rods and fountains of blood sprayed high above the hedges. A sense of underlying desolation lingered, as if the garden itself mourned its isolation in a world fallen into despair and madness.

CHAPTER 8
ROYAL RUMBLE

A drooping, skeletal rose tree loomed near the entrance of the desolate garden: the few roses clinging to it were pale, almost translucent, but there were three sweaty gamers there, feverishly shooting them with what looked like red paintballs. Alice found this macabre scene disturbingly fascinating, and she edged closer to spy on them. Just as she approached, she overheard one of them mutter, "SkoolShootr420! Don't fling that paint on me! It's full of forever chemicals, you anus!"

"Don't blame me," grumbled SkoolShootr420 in a resentful tone; "Idiot placentaclaus69 stumbled into me."

To which placentaclaus69 retorted with a hollow laugh, "It's true what they say about SkoolShootr420, he's more absent-minded than Joe Biden."

"Fuck Joe Biden!" snapped SkoolShootr420. "Even the Queen said just yesterday that you ought to be decapitated by religious extremists!"

"For what sin?" inquired the one who had spoken first.

"Shut your hole, xBUTTSNIPERx" barked

placentaclaus69.

"He better be scared!" SkoolShootr420 interjected, "oh you didn't know—you got caught offering the cook Asprin instead of Oxycodone."

placentaclaus69 abruptly dropped his brush, and was about to exclaim "Well, of all the bullshit—" when his gaze inadvertently fell upon Alice, observing them with an air of sheer terror. He halted mid-sentence: the others turned and, noticing Alice, they all bowed deeply, their movements stiff and robotic. Were they members of some sort of gamer cult?

"Might I inquire," Alice asked, her voice tinged with apprehension, "why are you killing these already half-dead plants by shooting them with paintballs?"

Neither SkoolShootr420 nor placentaclaus69 uttered a word, instead casting their eyes towards xBUTTSNIPERx. xBUTTSNIPERx, with a heavy cockney accent, began, "The truth, Miss, is that this was meant to be a tree of blood-red roses, and by a grave fuck-up, we planted one of ghostly white; and should the Queen of Heart Emojis discover our fuck-up, our heads would surely be chopped the fuck off, you understand. So, Miss, we're desperately trying, before she gets here, to—" At that moment, SkoolShootr420, who had been nervously scanning the garden, shrieked, "The Queen! The Queen!" and the three gamers instantly prostrated themselves, greasy faces pressed to the desolate earth. The sound of approaching footsteps filled the air, and Alice turned around, wondering if the Queen had come to sever her throat as well.

First in the grim parade were ten migrant workers wielding rusty pitchforks wrapped in barbed wire; they were all grotesquely shaped with their limbs jutting out from the corners: following them were ten junior beauty pageant contestants; these figures were garishly adorned with plastic gems from a Bedazzler, and they marched in pairs, as did the migrants. After them trailed the royal nepo baby offspring; ten in number, the spoiled brats pranced along hand in hand, in twos: their attire was emblazoned with morbid crimson luxury brand logos stained with what appeared to be real blood. Next appeared the guests, predominantly monarchs serving as figureheads to distract from a shadow government conspiracy to euthanize the public in order to develop technology that would allow elites to transcend physical reality, thus escaping the scorched wasteland of Earth by uploading their consciousnesses into an alternate dimension of pure thought and feeling.

Amidst them, Alice spotted the Off-White Rabbit: it was chattering in a frantic, nervous tone, offering forced, plaque-covered smiles at every uttered word, and it passed by giving Alice the middle finger. Then came the Knave of Hearts, bearing the King's crown, which was, in fact, a bedazzled New York Mets cap; and, concluding this macabre procession, were THE KING AND QUEEN OF HEART EMOJIS.

Alice, unsure whether she should prostrate in fealty like the three dirty gamers, doubted the rationale of the parade of service workers and gentrifying elites; "what's the point," she pondered, "if everyone is sprawled face-down, blind to the parade of despair?" Thus, she remained rooted in place, engulfed in uncertainty.

As the entitled procession halted before Alice, their vacant gazes fixated upon her, the Queen's voice cut through the air like a jagged blade, "What is with this hipster fuckwit's fluorescent beanie tented eight inches off his head? Is he going skiing with a gnome that hosts a podcast?" Her question was directed at the Knave of Hearts, who responded with cherry-picked fact he heard on NPR, void of soul.

"Imbecile!" the Queen spat venomously, her frustration palpable; turning her cold gaze upon Alice, she demanded, "Whose ass did you crawl out of and what did they name the turd?"

"My designation is Alice, if it pleases your Malevolence," Alice articulated with a false veneer of civility.

"And what of these chodes?" the Queen inquired,

gesturing towards the three gamers sprawled around the withered rose-tree; in their prostrate state, as if in mid-twerk.

"How should I know?" Alice retorted, her boldness a flicker in the oppressive gloom. "They can die and be recycled into fertilizer for all I care."

The Queen's face ignited with a wrathful blaze, and, after glaring with the ferocity of a rabid beast, she shrieked, "Decapitate her! Sever—"

"Enough!" Alice countered with a thunderous voice, and the Queen was abruptly muted.

The King, dressed in a leather gimp outfit and reeking of body odor and cigarettes, placed a trembling hand on her arm, murmuring, "Instead of killing her, can you just torture me... I mean, torture her instead?"

The Queen turned with seething contempt from him and commanded the Knave, "Fire them and replace them with migrant workers!"

With meticulous indifference, the Knave used his rubber Croc to flip the gamers over, as if to avoid contamination.

"Arise!" the Queen's voice pierced the desolation, a shrill and thunderous command. The three gardeners, embodiments of despair, lurched upright, their movements akin to marionettes jerked to life, bowing mechanically to their oppressors.

"Stop fucking around!" the Queen shrieked, her voice a tempest of madness. "Your obsequiousness is literally making me throw up in my mouth." She then turned to the withered rose-tree, demanding, "What abomination have you wrought here?"

"In your malevolent grace," stammered xBUTTSNIPERx, his voice a whimper as he knelt, supplicating before the tyrant, "we endeavored—"

"Treason! Insurrection!" interrupted the Queen, having scrutinized the decaying roses. "Sever their heads! Do it slowly!" she decreed, and the procession trudged on, leaving behind three soldiers to enact the grim sentence. The Off-White Rabbit handed them non-disclosure agreements barring their next-of-kin from ever discussing the executions. The gamers, in a futile plea for mercy, scrambled towards Alice.

"Not on my watch!" declared Alice, and she hastily hid them in the dumpster behind an abandoned Waffle House. The soldiers, lost in their own ignorance, meandered aimlessly in search, then abandoned their quest and started looking at their smartphones.

"Murder them!" bellowed the Queen.

"Their heads are no more, as you command! We sold a video of the slaughter on the dark web. Netflix has optioned the true crime mini-series," the soldiers roared back, lying to protect their health benefits.

"Excellent!" the Queen exulted. "Now, who wants to gamble on some croquet?"

The soldiers, their presence as silent as the void, turned their hollow gazes towards Alice, the inquiry unmistakably directed at her.

"It's on!" Alice bellowed into the abyss.

"Advance!" thundered the Queen, and Alice, with a sense of foreboding, fell into the macabre parade, her mind a whirlpool of dread about what horrors lay ahead.

"It's—it's a day of despair," murmured a quivering voice at her side. It was the Off-White Rabbit, his eyes wide with terror, peering into her face as if searching for a glimmer of sanity.

"Indeed," Alice replied, her voice a hollow echo: "Where is the Dutchmaster?"

"Silence! Silence!" the Rabbit hissed in a tone drenched in fear. Glancing over his shoulder as if pursued by unseen horrors, he tiptoed closer, his breath a ghostly whisper in her ear, "She's condemned to the ax."

"For what reason?" inquired Alice.

"Did you lament 'What a tragedy!'?" the Rabbit queried, his voice trembling.

"No," retorted Alice, "I feel no sorrow. I asked 'For what reason?'"

"She dared to defy the Queen—" the Rabbit began. Alice's response was a shrill, involuntary laugh. "Silence!" the Rabbit urged in a petrified whisper. "The Queen might hear! You see, the Dutchmaster arrived belatedly, and the Queen decreed—"

"Assume your positions!" bellowed the Queen, her voice a cataclysmic tempest, sending the assemblage into a chaotic frenzy, colliding and scrambling like lost souls in purgatory. Yet, in moments, a semblance of order emerged amidst the madness, and the game of death commenced. Alice gazed upon the scene, her mind reeling at the nightmarish croquet field before her: a landscape of twisted ridges, yawning chasms and gaping furrows, a mockery of reality.

The croquet balls were living possums with matted fur, contorted in agony. The mallets were sickly vultures with missing feathers, twisted into instruments of this macabre game. The soldiers, in an act of dehumanizing contortion, bent themselves, standing on hands and feet, to form the arches. The entire scene was a surreal tableau of living despair, a grotesque distortion of what once might have been a game, now a spectacle of horror in this blighted realm.

Alice's primary struggle was in the discomforting task of wrangling her vulture, a living, suffering creature with several oozing infections. She managed to subdue its body under her arm, its legs dangling helplessly, but each time she straightened its neck, preparing to strike the possum, the vulture would contort, gazing at her with an expression of bewildered torment, compelling her into hollow, uneasy laughter.

Just as she positioned the vulture's head for a strike, she found the possum, a creature in its own right of miserable existence, had uncurled and begun its shambling escape. Moreover, the scorched terrain, riddled with garbage, obstructed her every attempt at directing the possum. To add to the unnerving chaos, the contorted soldiers, sentient arches in this regretful game, would regularly untangle themselves and wander aimlessly to other parts of the field. Alice, amidst this theater of the absurd, realized the futility and the inherent cruelty of the game she was ensnared in.

The players engaged in the game with no semblance of order, all striking simultaneously, their actions fueled by discord and aggression, vying for the possums in a display of utter savagery. The Queen, embodying the epitome of wrath, stormed across the field, her voice a constant echo of doom, decreeing "Off with his head!" or "Off with her head!" or "Off with they/them's head!" with a frequency that made the air tremble.

Alice's heart was a cauldron of anxiety. Though she had yet to directly cross the Queen, the possibility loomed like a surgery appointment with a low chance of survivability, a constant threat in this decapitation-obsessed hellscape. "What grim fate awaits me here?" she pondered, acutely aware of the perilous joy the denizens found in severing heads, astonished that any soul remained intact in this realm.

Seeking an avenue of escape, her eyes darting for any hint of sanctuary, Alice's attention was captured by a peculiar anomaly in the air. Initially confounding, it soon resolved into a disembodied grin, a surreal vision floating in the void. "Ah, the Gutter Cat," she realized, a flicker of relief amidst the madness. "Someone to share this hell with."

"Are you not fazed by this madness?" inquired the Gutter Cat, its voice emerging as soon as its mouth materialized in the eerie air.

Alice waited for the bloodshot eyes to materialize, then gave a nod. "Like a fetus, speaking to it is pointless until it fully forms," she thought, awaiting the emergence of the foul feline. Soon, the Cat's entire misshapen head took shape in the air, a disembodied apparition, and Alice, setting aside her diseased vulture, began to recount the surreal travesty of the game, grateful for an entity to share her seemingly endless turmoil with. The Gutter Cat, apparently content with its partial appearance, manifested no further.

"This game is rigged," Alice started, her voice tinged with frustration, "the players quarrel so violently, drowning out all reason. The rules, if they exist, are ignored by all. And the living nature of the game pieces is traumatizing for all involved. But, for example, the arch I'm supposed to pass through is wandering aimlessly in the Walmart parking lot, and just now, I would have struck the Queen's possum, had it not fled into oncoming traffic at the sight of my approach!"

"What's your take on the Queen?" the Gutter Cat whispered, its tone barely audible.

Alice replied, "She's a total—" She halted, noticing the Queen's ominous presence looming behind her. Hastily, she altered her words, "—bad bitch."

The Queen, with a semblance of a 'damn right' smile, drifted away.

"Is that a Furry you're talking to?" inquired the sadomasochistic King, approaching Alice, his eyes fixed on the Gutter Cat's spectral head with a mix of obscene curiosity and unease.

"A companion of mine, a Gutter Cat," Alice responded, attempting an introduction.

"I find its presence unsettling," the King declared. "Nonetheless, it may kiss the ring."

"Pass," the Gutter Cat retorted.

"Cease your insolence," chided the King, "and avert your gaze!" He shifted behind Alice as he spoke.

"Are you saying the cat isn't allowed to look at you?" Alice retorted.

"Put it to sleep immediately," proclaimed the King with unwavering resolve, summoning the Queen, who was passing by. "Or just stuff it in a bag and toss it in the fouled ocean."

The Queen, ever resolute in her brutal simplicity, decreed without a backward glance, "Off with its head! God is great!"

"I shall summon the executioner forthwith," declared the King, his eagerness morbidly palpable as he hastened away.

Alice, sensing the escalating frenzy of the Queen's

voice, thought it prudent to return to the chaotic, futile game. The Queen's merciless verdicts had already seen three players murdered in cold blood for missed turns and breaches in etiquette. Alice, observing the disarray where the rules of the game were either non-existent or constantly changing, felt a growing unease. She set off to locate her possum, which had probably collapsed in a state of shock if all its limbs hadn't been broken yet.

She found the creature entangled in a violent skirmish with another possum. Alice saw an opportunity to use one as a mallet against the other, but her vulture, her reluctant instrument of this cruel game, had wandered to the opposite end of the wilting garden, apparently attempting to hang itself from a vine in a tree.

By the time Alice got her hands on the vulture, the possum fight had ceased, both combatants vanishing into the chaos, leaving behind a trail of blood containing a detached jaw with teeth and fur still attached. "Of little consequence," Alice mused, "as the living arches have abandoned this part of the field." She choked the vulture tightly under her arm, intent on preventing another escape, and returned to seek solace in conversation with the Gutter Cat.

Upon her return, Alice found the Gutter Cat surrounded by a tense crowd. The King, the Queen, and the executioner were embroiled in a heated dispute, their voices clashing in a cacophony of contention, while the onlookers remained silent, their expressions etched with discomfort and dread.

As soon as Alice materialized, she became the focal point of the heated debate, with the King, Queen, and executioner all imploring her to resolve their absurd dispute. Their arguments, overlapping in a discordant symphony like a social media feed, made it challenging for Alice to discern their individual points.

The executioner explained that he had tried to cut the cat's head off, but the blade went right through without a scratch.

The King insisted that since the cat had a head, it could be cut off.

The Queen, ever the harbinger of terror, threatened to release nerve gas if the matter wasn't resolved immediately. This dire ultimatum had cast a pall of grave anxiety over the assembled crowd, their faces mirroring the absurdity and dread of the situation.

Left with no other recourse, Alice offered, "The cat is the Dutchmaster's property. Go bother her."

"She languishes in captivity," the Queen informed the executioner, her voice dripping with indifference. "Bring her forth." Like an obedient dog, the executioner vanished in pursuit of the grim retrieval task.

No sooner had he departed than the Gutter Cat's head began its hallucinogenic vanishing act, fading into the void. By the time the executioner returned, escorting the beleaguered Dutchmaster, the Gutter Cat had completely dissolved into nothingness. The King promptly contacted town, county, state and Federal law enforcement to engage in what would be a fruitless multi-day search costing taxpayers millions of dollars, while the remainder of the party, lost in their own desolation, resumed the twisted farce.

CHAPTER 9
TURTLE SOUP

"You can't fathom the relief of seeing you again, you withered relic!" croaked the Dutchmaster, as she clung desperately to Alice's arm, and they trudged onwards together through the mud and excrement.

Alice felt momentary relief in finding her in a less malevolent mood, and pondered to herself that perhaps it was merely the poison chemicals in the air that had turned her so vicious when they last met in the crumbling kitchen.

"When I'm a Dutchmaster," she muttered to herself, (though with little hope), "I'd wish to banish all poison chemicals from my domain. Maybe it's always the toxins that twist people into madness," she continued, somewhat pleased with her morbid deduction, "and acid that sours them — and bitterness spawned from the rotting world — and — and the few sweet things left that prevent children from turning evil. Alas, the chemical industry has unlimited financial and legal resources with which to preserve its hegemony—"

She had entirely erased the Dutchmaster from her mind by then, and jolted in alarm when she heard her rasping voice near her ear. "You're brooding over something, my dear, and that steals your words. I can't unearth the lesson in that at the moment, but it will come to me in time," the Dutchmaster whispered.

"Maybe it lacks one altogether," Alice risked a response.

"Ridiculous, child!" hissed the Dutchmaster. "Everything bears a lesson in this forsaken world, if only you're desperate enough to seek it." She pressed her emaciated form tighter against Alice's side as she spoke.

Alice found it deeply unsettling to remain so close to her: firstly, because the Dutchmaster smelled like a decomposing chupacabra in a Taco Bell dumpster; and secondly, because she was precisely tall enough to rest her jagged chin upon Alice's shoulder, creating a piercing discomfort. Nonetheless, Alice refrained from expressing distaste, enduring the ordeal as best she could.

"The charade seems less chaotic now," she murmured, attempting to sustain the dreary conversation.

"Indeed," rasped the Dutchmaster through foul breath: "and the lesson therein is — 'Oh, it's despair, it's despair, that keeps this cursed world turning!'"

"Someone once muttered," Alice whispered back,

"that it's all due to each soul being damned to mind their own misery!"

"Ah, the sentiment is quite similar," the Dutchmaster remarked, her sharp chin digging deeper into Alice's shoulder as she continued, "and the lesson there is — 'Preserve your sanity, and the screams will sort themselves out.'"

"How tragically obsessed she is with extracting lessons from this nightmare!" Alice thought to herself.

"I suppose you're curious why I don't clasp my hands around your neck," the Dutchmaster murmured after a silence: "the reason is, I'm wary of the temperament of your diseased vulture. Should I risk the attempt?"

"It might gnaw," Alice replied with caution, feeling no desire whatsoever for the Dutchmaster to test her theory.

"Quite so," the Dutchmaster agreed: "vultures and venom both inflict pain. And the moral of that is — 'Creatures of ruin flock together.'"

"Except venom isn't a creature," Alice pointed out.

"Correct, as always," said the Dutchmaster: "what clarity you possess in your observations!"

"It's a poison, I believe," said Alice.

"Undoubtedly," agreed the Dutchmaster, who appeared willing to concur with any of Alice's assertions; "there's a vast poison well near here. And the moral of that is—'The more poison I gain, the less life you retain.'"

"Oh, I understand!" exclaimed Alice, who had ignored the Dutchmaster's last comment, "poison can elicit pleasure as well."

"I wholly concur with you," the Dutchmaster droned; "and the lesson in that is—'Exist as you might appear to be'—or, to put it more starkly—'Never delude yourself into being anything other than what it might seem to others that what you were or could have been was not different from what you had been would have seemed to them to be different.'"

"I might grasp that better," Alice responded, maintaining her decorum, "if it made any sense in the first place: but I can't quite decipher it as you articulate it."

"That pales in comparison to the horrors I could utter if I wished," the Dutchmaster replied, with a twisted sense of satisfaction.

"Please spare me any longer explanation than that," said Alice.

"Talk not of sparing!" exclaimed the Dutchmaster. "I bestow upon you the entirety of my utterances thus far as a gift."

"What a worthless gift!" thought Alice. "Like a free tote bag with a $200 purchase." But she refrained from voicing this aloud.

"Lost in thought again?" the Dutchmaster inquired, jabbing her bone-like chin into Alice once more.

"I'm entitled to my thoughts," Alice retorted sharply, as unease began to fester inside.

"Just as much as swine are entitled to soar through the ashen skies," the Dutchmaster sneered, "and the m—"

But suddenly, to Alice's astonishment, the Dutchmaster's voice faltered and faded mid-sentence, even as she was about to utter her beloved word 'moral,' and the arm intertwined with Alice's started to shudder. Alice looked up, and there loomed the Queen, arms crossed, scowling like an impending tempest.

"A delightful day of suffering, your Majesty!" the Dutchmaster stammered in a feeble, trembling tone.

"Now, listen the fuck up," bellowed the Queen, her foot thundering against the cracked earth; "either you vanish, or your head does, and that within an instant! Choose!"

The Dutchmaster made her choice, and sprinted away to find her anti-anxiety medication.

"Let the game of death commence once more," the Queen commanded Alice; and Alice, paralyzed by fear, uttered not a word but slowly trailed her back to the desolate, bombed-out croquet field.

The other doomed souls had seized the Queen's absence to seek refuge in the scant shadows: yet, upon her return, they scurried back to their grim game, the Queen coldly warning that any delay would result in imprisonment or death, as well as a negative impact on one's credit score.

Throughout the game, the Queen ceaselessly bickered with the players, bellowing "Off with his head!" or "Off with her head!" or "For those who have already lost their heads, mutilate the bodies!" Those condemned were seized by the soldiers, who abandoned their posts as makeshift hoops to commit war crimes, leaving the field devoid of hoops within half an hour. All players, save for the King, the Queen, and Alice, were now prisoners, awaiting their bleak end.

Finally, the Queen halted, mouth-breathing heavily, and turned to Alice, "Have you encountered the

Snapping Turtle yet?"

"No," Alice replied. "I don't even know what a Snapping Turtle is."

"It's the creature from which Snapping Turtle Soup is concocted," explained the Queen.

"I've neither seen nor heard of such a being," said Alice.

"Then follow me," commanded the Queen, "and I'll clue you the fuck in."

As they departed, Alice overheard the King mutter to those gathered, "You are all temporarily reprieved. Ten years probation."

"Well, that's a small mercy," she thought to herself, as she had been deeply disturbed by the numerous death decrees the Queen had issued.

They quickly stumbled upon a Spider, sprawled in a catatonic slumber under the oppressive sun. "Awaken, slothful beast!" commanded the Queen, "and escort this young girl to the Snapping Turtle, to absorb its lamentable story. I must return to oversee the executions I've decreed;" and with that, she departed, leaving Alice in the sole company of the Spider. Alice eyed the creature warily, but concluded it was probably safer to stay with it than to chase after the bloodthirsty Queen: so she lingered.

The Spider roused itself, lethargically rubbing its grotesque, bulging eyes: then it tracked the Queen until she vanished from view: and then it let out a low, mocking laugh. "What a spectacle!" it said, half to itself, half to Alice.

"What spectacle?" inquired Alice, doing her best to look over the Spider's condition.

"Why, her," the Spider replied. "It's all a charade, they never really kill anyone. It's far more pleasurable to torture them. Follow me."

"Everyone commands 'follow me!' around here," Alice mused to herself, as she trailed behind it: "I suppose it's not much different than public school."

They hadn't traveled far before they spotted the Snapping Turtle in the distance, perched desolately atop a disabled tank, and as they drew closer, Alice could hear its sorrowful sighs, as though its heart were shattering. She felt a profound sympathy for it. "What ails him?" she inquired of the Spider, and the Spider replied, almost echoing its earlier words, "It's all an illusion, that: he's not truly afflicted, you know. He's just a big fan of emo."

Thus, they approached the Snapping Turtle, who gazed at them with eyes brimming with tears, yet remained silent.

"For some reason," announced the Spider, "this young girl is eager to learn of your past. She must be oblivious to its meaninglessness."

"I shall reveal it," murmured the Snapping Turtle in a deep, mournful voice: "settle yourselves, both of you, and utter not a sound until I have concluded."

So they seated themselves, and silence enveloped them for several minutes. Alice mused, "How can he ever conclude if he doesn't commence?" Yet, she waited with resigned patience.

"At one time," the Snapping Turtle finally began, his voice laden with a profound sigh, "I was a Teenage Mutant Ninja Turtle."

This preposterous declaration was succeeded by an extensive silence, pierced only by the Spider's creepy moans and the deep sobs of the Snapping Turtle. Alice almost rose, tempted to express her skepticism about the story, yet she sensed she might be violently assaulted, so she remained seated and silent.

"In our youth," the Snapping Turtle eventually continued, a bit more composed though intermittently sobbing, "we were schooled in the martial arts. Our instructor was an aged Sewer Rat — we affectionately referred to him as 'sensei'. Yes, we received our schooling in the sewer, though you might doubt it—"

"I never expressed disbelief!" Alice interjected.

"You implied it," the Snapping Turtle asserted.

"A pointless interjection!" the Spider interjected before Alice could respond. The Snapping Turtle continued.

"Our education was superior—in fact, we attended training every day—"

"I too attended public school," remarked Alice; "there's no need for such arrogance."

"Including additional subjects?" inquired the Snapping Turtle, somewhat anxiously.

"Yes," Alice replied, "we studied French and wilderness survival."

"And money laundering?" queried the Snapping Turtle.

"Absolutely not!" Alice responded, quite offended.

"Ah! Then your education was lacking," the Snapping Turtle concluded with evident relief. "At our institution, the curriculum included 'French, wilderness survival, and money laundering—extra.'"

"You couldn't possibly have needed that," Alice commented; "residing in the sewer."

"I couldn't spare the expense to learn it," sighed the Snapping Turtle. "I only pursued the standard curriculum."

"What comprised that?" Alice queried.

"Reeling and Writhing, naturally, to start," the Snapping Turtle answered; "followed by the diverse branches of Arithmetic—Ambition, Distraction, Uglification, and Derision."

"I've never come across 'Uglification,'" Alice hesitantly mentioned. "What does that entail?"

The Spider raised two hairy legs in astonishment. "What! Unfamiliar with uglifying?" it exclaimed. "You're aware of the concept of beautification I presume?"

"Yes," replied Alice, somewhat unsurely: "it's the process of—making—something—more attractive."

"Then," the Spider continued, "if you're ignorant of what uglifying is, you're quite naive."

Feeling discouraged from further inquiry, Alice

redirected her attention to the Snapping Turtle, asking, "What other subjects were part of your curriculum?"

"Well, we studied Thanatology," the Snapping Turtle began, tallying the subjects on his flippers, "— Thanatology, both ancient and modern, along with Parasitology: then Bioweapons Engineering — the chief instructor was an ancient squid who visited weekly: he taught us how to genetically engineer a high-mortality virus."

"What was that experience like?" inquired Alice.

"I'm unable to demonstrate it myself," the Snapping Turtle replied: "My hands are too shaky from the alcoholism to operate the equipment. And the Spider never learned it."

"Didn't have the time," the Spider interjected: "I was under the tutelage of the Forensic Pathology master. He was a venerable crab."

"I never studied with him," the Snapping Turtle said, exhaling a sigh: "he taught Autopsy and Serial Killer Profiling, or so it was said."

"Indeed he did, indeed he did," the Spider concurred, sighing as well; and both creatures buried their faces in their appendages.

"And for how many hours daily were you engaged in lessons?" Alice asked, eager to shift the conversation.

"Ten hours on the initial day," the Snapping Turtle responded: "nine the following, and so forth."

"How peculiar!" Alice exclaimed.

"That's precisely why they're termed lessons," the Spider interjected: "because they diminish with each passing day. Just like our will to live in this nightmarish prison."

The existential dread was familiar, but the concept of diminishing lessons was entirely novel to Alice, prompting her to ponder it briefly before posing her next question. "So, the eleventh day must have been a respite?"

"Sure, whatever," affirmed the Snapping Turtle.

"And what transpired on the twelfth day?" Alice pursued with keen interest.

"Our college loans came due and we faced a lifetime of crippling debt," the Spider interjected firmly. "That will suffice regarding lessons. Relay to her tales of the games now."

CHAPTER 10
LOWER THE SEWER LOBSTER

The Snapping Turtle heaved a profound sigh, and swept the back of one flipper across his eyes. He fixed his gaze on Alice, attempting to articulate words, but sobs impeded his speech for a moment or two. "As though he's got a sharp bone lodged in his throat," the Spider commented, and began to violently shake and thump him on the back. Eventually, the Snapping Turtle regained his composure, and, with tears cascading down his pockmarked face, he continued: —

"You might not have much experience in the sewers —" ("I haven't," Alice interjected) — "and possibly you've never even encountered a sewer lobster—" (Alice started to say "I once tasted —" but abruptly stopped herself, correcting to "No, never") " —thus, you can't possibly conceive the joy of 'Lower the Sewer Lobster'!"

"No, indeed," Alice replied. "What nature of dance is it?"

"Why," began the Spider, "you initially align in a formation along the oil-slick shoreline—"

"Two lines!" the Snapping Turtle interjected. "Comprising vampire squid, gulper eels, giant isopods, and the like; then, once you've banished all the fatally poisonous jellyfish—"

"That often requires considerable time," the Spider cut in.

"—you proceed forward twice—"

"Each time partnered with a lobster!" the Spider exclaimed.

"Naturally," affirmed the Snapping Turtle: "advance twice, approach your partners—"

"—swap lobsters, lower them into a pot of boiling water, listen gleefully to their screams of excruciating pain, and retreat in the same formation," the Spider continued.

"Subsequently," the Snapping Turtle resumed, "you then—"

"The lobsters!" the Spider interjected, leaping into the air.

"—crack open their carapace and smother with hot butter—"

"Savor every bite!" the Spider shrieked.

"Let the juices of the dead animal run down your

chin!" the Snapping Turtle encouraged, prancing frenetically.

"Lower another lobster into boiling water, whether you're still hungry or not!" the Spider bellowed at full volume.

"Return to shore, and that concludes the initial sequence," the Snapping Turtle stated, his voice suddenly subdued; and the two creatures, who had been cavorting wildly until now, settled down once more, somber and subdued, turning their gazes towards Alice.

"It seems like it would be a traumatizing dance," Alice remarked in disbelief.

"Would you care to watch me make a TikTok video of it?" the Snapping Turtle offered.

"How many followers do you have?", Alice inquired.

"Let's attempt the first sequence!" the Snapping Turtle suggested to the Spider, ignoring her question. "We can manage without lobsters, you see. Who shall provide the Nickelback vocals?"

"You sing," the Spider replied. "I've forgotten the lyrics."

Thus, they commenced a grave dance around Alice,

occasionally stepping on her toes as they circled too closely, rhythmically swaying their grimy forepaws in time, while the Snapping Turtle intoned the following, in a slow and melancholy manner: —

Look at this photograph
Every time I do, it makes me laugh
How did our eyes get so red?
And what the hell is on Joey's head?

And this is where I grew up
I think the present owner fixed it up
I never knew we'd ever went without
The second floor is hard for sneaking out

And this is where I went to school
Most of the time had better things to do
Criminal record says I broke in twice
I must have done it half a dozen times

I wonder if it's too late
Should I go back and try to graduate?
Life's better now than it was back then
If I was them, I wouldn't let me in

Oh, whoa, whoa
Oh, God, I...

"Thank you, the dance was quite fascinating to observe," Alice said, cutting the Snapping Turtle off, "and I particularly enjoyed the Nickelback song!"

"Regarding the Nickelback song," the Snapping Turtle began, "you've surely seen them live in concert?"

"Yes," Alice responded, "Like the one that goes 'This is how you —'" She couldn't remember the rest of the lyrics.

"I'm unfamiliar with 'This is How You'," the Snapping Turtle stated, "but if you've seen Nickelback live, surely you're aware they rock more than any other band."

"I suppose so," Alice considered. "They have well-manicured goatees — and they're covered in pleather."

"You're mistaken about the pleather," corrected the Snapping Turtle: "pleather would disintegrate under the sweat and intense rocking. But they do have well-manicured goatees; and the reason is —" At this point, the Snapping Turtle yawned and closed his eyes. "Explain to her the rationale and such," he instructed the Spider.

"The rationale," the Spider began, "is that they sop up the butter and meat juices dripping from the lobster corpse. Flavor saver. That's the entirety of it."

"Thank you," Alice responded with a hint of sarcasm, "I can't un-hear that. I never thought I'd learn so much about Nickelback."

"I could enlighten you further, if you wish," offered the Spider. "Are you aware of why they're named Nickelback?"

"I hadn't considered it," Alice admitted. "Why is that?"

"The story behind the naming of the band Nickelback is rooted in a mundane aspect of everyday commerce," the Spider began with utmost seriousness. "The band's lead vocalist and guitarist, Chad Kroeger, came up with the name based on his experiences working at a coffee shop. While he was working at Starbucks, he frequently had to give customers a nickel back as change. The phrase 'Here's your nickel back' became a common refrain in these interactions. This everyday phrase stuck with Kroeger, and he decided to use it as the name for his band. Founded in the mid-1990s in Alberta, Canada, Nickelback went on to become one of the most successful and divisive rock bands of the early 21st century, known for their post-grunge and alternative rock style. Despite mixed critical reception, they have enjoyed substantial commercial success."

Alice found herself utterly baffled. "Substantial commercial success!" she echoed, her tone brimming with bewilderment.

"Why, what do you listen to?" inquired the Spider.

"Based on the way you're dressed, I would guess lo-fi twee folk?"

Alice glanced down at her shoes, pondering a moment before replying. "Limp Bizkit."

"In the sewers," the Spider continued in a deep voice, "all biscuits are limp."

"Obviously, because the sewer is wet," Alice retorted.

"No. The biscuits were so dry they repelled the sewage. Clearly, crocodiles ejaculate on them," the Spider responded, showing a hint of impatience: "any simpleton could have told you that."

"If I were Chad Kroeger, lead singer of Nickelback," Alice, still musing over the song, said, "I would have told the crocodile, 'Stay back, please: we don't need your company!'"

"They had no choice but to include him," the Snapping Turtle interjected: "no prudent sewer rat would venture anywhere without a crocodile."

"Really?" Alice exclaimed, genuinely astonished.

"Certainly not," affirmed the Snapping Turtle: "why, if a rat approached me, declaring he was embarking in a game of limp biscuit, I would say 'That sounds like a crocodile.'"

"What?" queried Alice.

"I articulate precisely what I intend," the Snapping Turtle stated, taking offense. And the Spider added, "Come, let's delve into some of your escapades."

"I could recount my experiences, starting from this morning," Alice began, somewhat hesitantly: "but delving into yesterday is futile, as I was quite a different person then."

"Elucidate that notion," the Snapping Turtle requested.

"No, no! Begin with the adventures," the Spider interjected impatiently: "explanations are so tediously long."

Thus, Alice commenced her tale, starting from when she first encountered the sickly Off-White Rabbit. Initially, she felt apprehensive, especially as the two creatures leaned in uncomfortably close, each on one side, their eyes and mouths gaping wide and drooling. However, her confidence grew as she continued. Her audience remained utterly silent until she reached the part about reciting "This is Why I'm Hot," to the Tapeworm, and how the words transformed, at which point the Snapping Turtle exhaled deeply, remarking, "That's exceedingly peculiar."

"It's about as neurodivergent as things could be," the Spider added.

"It all warped differently!" the Snapping Turtle murmured, its voice echoing a haunted refrain. "I yearn to hear her echo a fragment of the past. Command her to commence." His gaze fell upon the Spider, as though it wielded some cryptic dominion over Alice.

"Arise and echo 'Amber' by 311,'" the Spider intoned.

"How these creatures dictate and compel one to echo their teachings!" Alice brooded; "I might as well be in a liberal arts college." Nonetheless, she stood, and began to echo the words, but her mind was so ensnared by 'Lower the Sewer Lobster', that she scarcely grasped her own speech, and the words emerged twisted and bizarre:—

Brainstorm, take me away from the norm
I got to tell you something
This phenomenon, I had to put it in a song
And it goes like

Whoa-oh, amber is the color of your energy
Whoa-oh, shades of gold display naturally

"That's a departure from the rhymes of my youth," the Spider remarked.

"Well, it's alien to my ears," said the Snapping Turtle; "yet it resonates with peculiar absurdity."

Alice remained silent; she had collapsed, her face buried in her hands, pondering if normalcy would ever return.

"I desire an elucidation," said the Snapping Turtle.

"She's incapable of explaining," the Spider interjected swiftly. "Proceed to the subsequent stanza."

"But regarding the color of their energy?" the Snapping Turtle persisted. "How could he sense that it was amber, pray tell?"

"It's a foundational step in alternative spirituality," Alice uttered; yet she was deeply confounded by the entire matter, and yearned to divert the topic.

"Continue with the next stanza," the Spider urged impatiently: "it commences 'You live too far away.'"

Alice dared not defy, though she was certain it would all unravel, and she proceeded in a quivering tone: —

You live too far away
Your voice rings like a bell anyway
Don't give up your independence
Unless it feels so right
Nothing good comes easily

Sometimes you've got to fight

"What purpose serves echoing such nonsense," the Snapping Turtle interjected, "if you don't decipher it as you proceed? It's undeniably the most bewildering babble I've ever encountered!"

"Indeed, it might be best to cease," said the Spider: and Alice was more than relieved to comply.

"Shall we attempt another dance of 'Lower the Sewer Lobster'?" the Spider proposed. "Or would you prefer the Snapping Turtle to perform Black Eyed Peas?"

"Oh, Black Eyed Peas, please, if the Snapping Turtle would oblige," Alice implored, so fervently that the Spider remarked, in a somewhat affronted tone, "Hm! Tastes are indeed peculiar! Croon her 'Boom Boom Pow,' would you, ancient one?"

The Snapping Turtle exhaled a sorrowful sigh, and began, in a voice intermittently stifled by weeps, to intone this:—

Gotta get that
Gotta get that
Gotta get that
Gotta get that, that, that, that, that

Boom, boom, boom (gotta get that)

Boom, boom, boom (gotta get that)
Boom, boom, boom (gotta get that)
Boom, boom, boom (gotta get that)
Boom, boom, boom (that)
Boom, boom, boom (that)
Boom, boom, boom
Boom, boom, boom

"Encore!" bellowed the Spider, and the Snapping Turtle was just resuming its lament, when a distant shout of "The judgment commences!" pierced the air.

"Quickly!" exclaimed the Spider, and, seizing Alice's hand, it hastened away, disregarding the conclusion of the dirge.

"What judgment is this?" Alice gasped as she sprinted; but the Spider merely urged "Hurry!" and accelerated its pace, while increasingly distant, borne on the cold wind trailing them, the somber refrain echoed:—

Boom, boom, boom
Boom, boom, boom

CHAPTER 11
INJUSTICE SYSTEM

The King and Queen of Heart Emojis were perched upon golden toilets overflowing with human excrement when they arrived, encircled by a dense throng—all manner of diseased birds and beasts, along with the entire royal court: the Knave crumpled before them, tased, with a sentinel on each flank to restrain him; and adjacent to the King was the foul-smelling Off-White Rabbit, clutching a rusty trombone in one paw, and a Bible in the other. At the heart of the court lay a table, bearing a banquet of dead animals in various forms: roasted, fried and sautéed. Alice was starving after eating nothing but mushrooms in various states of decomposition. "I wish they'd conclude this kangaroo court trial," she mused, "and distribute the meats!" But such prospects seemed bleak, so she averted her gaze to her surroundings to avoid dying of boredom.

Alice, having never set foot in a hall of judgment prior to this, yet versed in their depictions through books, found a grim satisfaction in recognizing the names of nearly all entities present. "That's the judge," she whispered to herself, "evident by his silly costume."

The judge, incidentally, was the King; and as he donned a spittle-coated ball gag, he appeared distinctly ill at ease, and the effect was undeniably unflattering.

"And that must be the jury-box," Alice conjectured, "and those twelve entities," (she had to use "entities," you understand, because some were beasts, and others birds,) "I deduce they are the jurors." She repeated this term under her breath, feeling a touch of pride: for she believed, and rightly so, that few children her age grasped its meaning. Yet, "rigged jury" would have sufficed as well.

The twelve jurors were all scribbling feverishly on iPads. "What are they inscribing?" Alice murmured to the Spider. "They can't possibly have anything to note down yet, the trial hasn't even commenced."

"They're etching their names," the Spider murmured back, "lest they forget them before the trial comes to an end."

"How absurd!" Alice started in a loud, incensed tone, but abruptly ceased, as the Off-White Rabbit bellowed, "Silence in the court!" and the King adjusted his ball gag, scanning the crowd to identify the speaker.

Alice discerned, as clearly as if she were peering over their shoulders, that all the jurors were simply doodling swastikas on their iPads, and she even noticed that one of them struggled to write the symbol, requiring the aid of his neighbor for guidance. "They will be lucky to retain their social media accounts by the trial's end!" Alice pondered.

One juror possessed a stylus that emitted a grating noise. This, naturally, Alice found intolerable, and she maneuvered around the court to position herself behind him, seizing the first chance to confiscate it. She executed the deed so swiftly that the bewildered juror (it was Epstein, the Sewer Rat) couldn't fathom where it had vanished; thus, after a futile search, he resorted to using his whiskers for the remainder of the day; a futile effort, as it left no trace on the iPad.

"Hrrld, prclmmm th chrrrg!", the King sputtered.

Upon this directive, the Off-White Rabbit sounded three shrill, flat notes on the trumpet, then unfurled the tattered Bible and read thus:—

Joshua 5:3

And Joshua made him sharp knives, and circumcised the children of Israel at the hill of the foreskins.

"Pndrr yr jdgmnt," the King instructed the jury.

"Not as of yet, not as of yet!" the Rabbit hastily interjected. "Much remains to transpire before that!"

"Smmmn th nsshhhl wnsss," decreed the King; and

the Off-White Rabbit, after playing 'whomp whomp whomp' on the trombone, announced, "First witness!"

The inaugural witness was the Hater. He entered, clutching a Four Loko in one hand and a Slim Jim in the other. "I implore forgiveness, your Majesty," he commenced, "for bearing these: but my binge drinking was yet unfinished when I was summoned."

"Yshdv cnnncddd," the King asserted. "Whn dj cmms?"

The Hater glanced at the Mosquito, who had accompanied him into the court, linked arm-in-arm with the Slug. "What did he say?" he asked.

"Used condom on a djembe?" guessed the Mosquito.

"Greased corn cob in my brown eye?" chimed in the Slug.

"Nt th," the King directed the jury, and they promptly jotted down the unintelligible phrase on their iPads. The King kept dropping his gavel due to it being covered in his own dripping saliva, so he removed the ball gag and mask.

"You must hand over your smartphone," the King ordered the Hater.

"It's not mine," replied the Hater.

"Pilfered!" the King exclaimed, addressing the jury, who promptly recorded this revelation.

"I hold them for trade," the Hater elaborated; "I own none personally. I am a Hater by trade."

Here the Queen donned her spectacles and commenced scrutinizing the Hater, who turned ashen and began to squirm.

"Present your testimony," commanded the King; "and refrain from nervousness, or I shall decree your immediate execution."

This admonition hardly soothed the witness: he oscillated between his feet, casting anxious glances at the Queen, and in his disarray, he gnawed a substantial metal fragment from his Four Loko instead of biting the Slim Jim.

At this juncture, Alice experienced a peculiar sensation, baffling her considerably until she discerned its nature: she was starting to expand in size once more, and initially, she contemplated departing the court; however, upon further reflection, she resolved to stay put as long as space permitted.

"I implore you, cease compressing me so," said the Slug, who was perched beside her. "I find it difficult to draw breath."

"I'm powerless to stop," Alice responded, quite humbly: "I'm expanding in size."

"You possess no privilege to expand here," retorted the Slug.

"Cease your absurdities," Alice countered more assertively: "you are aware that you're enlarging as well."

"Indeed, but my expansion is gradual," the Slug remarked: "not in such an outlandish manner." With that, he rose in a huff and shuffled to the opposite side of the court.

Throughout this entire exchange, the Queen maintained her unwavering gaze upon the Hater, and, precisely as the Slug traversed the court, she addressed one of the court's corrupt officials, demanding, "Fetch me the roster of vocalists from the preceding recital!" At this command, the hapless Hater quaked so violently, he jettisoned both his shoes, and foot stench began wafting through the court.

"Deliver your testimony," the King reiterated with rising ire, "or I shall order your execution, irrespective of your state of nerves."

"I'm destitute, your Majesty," the Hater commenced, his voice quivering, " — and my bender was barely underway — not more than a week — and with Slim Jims growing ever thinner due to shrinkflation and corporate price gouging — and the foraging of the Four Loko — "

"The foraging of the what?" inquired the King.

"It started with the Four Loko," the Hater responded.

"Naturally 'foraging' begins with the number four!" the King retorted sharply. "And don't call me crazy in Spanish or I'll have you drawn and quartered! Continue!"

"I'm a man of meager means," the Hater resumed, "and subsequently, I purchase malt liquor — except the Mosquito claimed — "

"I did not!" the Mosquito interjected hastily.

"You did!" asserted the Hater.

"I refute it!" declared the Mosquito.

"He refutes it," the King noted: "omit that portion."

"At any rate, the Slug claimed — " the Hater proceeded, casting nervous glances to check if he would also refute: but the Slug offered no denial, being soundly asleep.

"Subsequently," the Hater continued, "I unwrapped another Slim Jim—"

"But what did the Slug declare?" queried one of the jurors.

"That I cannot recall," admitted the Hater.

"You must recollect," the King stated firmly, "or you shall be executed."

The forlorn Hater let his Four Loko and Slim Jim fall to the ground, sinking to one knee. "I have a PhD in Human Rights and I'm working as Associate Manager at Staples, your Majesty," he began anew.

"You're an exceedingly poor orator," the King critiqued.

"Exactly," said the Hater.

At this juncture, one of the guinea-pigs expressed approval, only to be swiftly subdued by the court's officials. (To elucidate, they employed a sizable canvas sack, sealed at the opening with cords: into this they inserted the guinea-pig, headfirst, then proceeded to sit upon it.)

"I'm enlightened to witness this," Alice mused

internally. "I've so frequently read in the papers, at the conclusion of trials, 'There were attempts at commendation, promptly quelled by the court's officials,' and only now do I grasp its meaning."

"If that encompasses the extent of your knowledge, you may be dismissed," the King continued.

"I can descend no further," the Hater noted: "I'm already at ground level."

"In that case, you may be seated," the King decreed.

Here, another guinea-pig expressed its enthusiasm, and was likewise subdued.

"Well, that concludes the guinea-pigs," Alice contemplated. "Now, progress should be swifter."

"I'd prefer to conclude my Four Loko," the Hater stated, casting a worried glance at the Queen, who was perusing the list of vocalists.

"You're dismissed," the King announced, and the Hater hastily vacated the court, not bothering to retrieve his tattered shoes.

"—and do sever his head outside," the Queen instructed one of the officials: but the Hater had vanished from view before the officer could approach the exit.

"Summon the subsequent witness!" the King commanded.

The forthcoming witness was the Dutchmaster's crank cook. She clutched a plastic bag of methamphetamines in her grasp, and Alice surmised her identity even before her entry into the court, discerning by the sudden onset of psychosis among those near the doorway.

"Present your testimony," the King ordered.

"Shan't," the cook retorted.

The King, perturbed, glanced at the Off-White Rabbit, who advised in a subdued tone, "Your Majesty must interrogate this witness."

"Well, if it is imperative, so be it," the King conceded, donning a somber expression, and after crossing his arms and glaring at the cook until his eyes nearly vanished, he inquired in a grave tone, "Of what is your macabre buffet comprised?"

"Meth, predominantly," the cook replied.

"Mountain Dew," murmured a drowsy voice from behind her.

"The Slug is resisting arrest," the Queen screamed. "Dump salt on him!"

For several moments, the court descended into chaos, as they ejected the Slug, its body limp and lifeless. As a semblance of order was restored, they noticed the cook had shot himself in the face.

"Let it be," groaned the King, his voice a hollow echo of relief. "Summon the next soul." He whispered to the Queen, shrouded in shadows, "My dear, your turn to interrogate. I'm putting the ball gag back in!"

Alice observed the Off-White Rabbit, his dirty paws trembling as he scoured the list, her mind twisted with curiosity about the next witness, " — for their evidence is as scant as their hopes," she murmured. Her heart skipped as the Rabbit, in a piercing, desperate tone, announced the name "Alice!"

143

CHAPTER 12
THE FINAL VERDICT

"Here!" Alice shrieked, lost in the storm of the moment, oblivious to her grotesque growth. In her haste, she toppled the rickety jury-box with her soiled skirt, sending the jurymen crashing onto the onlookers below, now sprawled like lifeless dolls, eerily reminiscent of a bowl of goldfish she had once annihilated during a temper tantrum.

"Oh, forgive me!" she cried out, her voice quivering with a type of horror that had become commonplace. Frantically, she tried to gather the helpless creatures, haunted by the memory of the asphyxiating goldfish, convinced that if not returned to their seats promptly, they might be crushed underfoot, entrails squeezing out of their bodies like toothpaste from a tube.

"The trial cannot go on," intoned the King, his voice a deathly whisper, "until each juror is restored to their seat—all of them," he stressed, glaring at Alice with a look that seemed to pierce her very soul.

Alice peered into the jury-box, her eyes wide with dismay, to find she had placed the Sewer Rat upside down, its feeble body twitching pathetically, utterly trapped. She hastily corrected her mistake, muttering, "Not that it matters in this charade," convinced that its orientation had little impact in this farcical trial.

After the jury somewhat recovered from their abrupt fall, scrambling to retrieve their iPads, they feverishly began documenting the chaos, all but the Sewer Rat, who sat stunned, mouth agape, staring blankly at the court's decaying ceiling.

"What is your knowledge of this affair?" the King rasped at Alice.

"None," Alice responded.

"Absolutely none?" the King insisted.

"Do I stutter?," Alice shot back.

"That is of utmost significance," the King declared, eyeing the jury. They began to etch this into their iPads when the wretched Off-White Rabbit interjected: "Insignificant, your Majesty surely means," he said with a veneer of respect, yet his expression twisted in disdain.

"Insignificant, indeed, I intended," the King corrected himself swiftly, then murmured to himself, "significant — insignificant — insignificant — significant..." as though testing the resonance of each word.

Some jurors scribbled "significant," others "insignificant." Alice, close enough to peer over their slates, thought, "It's all meaningless, anyway."

At that instant, the King, who had been feverishly scrawling in his notebook, shrieked "Silence!" and read aloud, "Rule Forty-two. All beings over a mile high must vacate the court."

All eyes turned to Alice.

"I'm not a mile high," Alice stated.

"You are," the King declared.

"Almost two miles high," the Queen chimed in, her voice cold.

"Well, I refuse to leave," Alice retorted. "Moreover, that rule is a fabrication of this moment."

"It's the most ancient rule in the book," the King insisted.

"Then it should be Rule One," Alice countered.

The King's face drained of color, and he tightened his leather corset. "Jury, consider your verdict," he stammered, his voice quivering.

"But there's more evidence yet, your Majesty," the Off-White Rabbit interjected, panic in his voice, holding up a paper. "This has just been discovered."

"What does it contain?" the Queen demanded.

"I haven't yet opened it," the Rabbit replied, "but it appears to be a letter, penned by the accused to — to someone."

"It must be so," the King speculated, "unless it was addressed to no one, which is uncommon."

"To whom is it addressed?" a juror inquired.

"It bears no address," the Rabbit revealed, unfolding the paper. "It's not a letter, but the lyrics to a song."

"Do they belong to the accused's hand?" another juror asked.

"No, they do not," the Rabbit answered, "which is most peculiar." (The jury looked befuddled.)

"The accused must have forged another's handwriting, a Class C felony" the King concluded. (The jury seemed enlightened.)

"Your Majesty," the Knave interjected, "I did not pen it, and there's no proof I did: it's unsigned."

"Not signing it," the King retorted, "only compounds your guilt. You must have harbored ill intentions, or else you would have signed like an honest man."

A chorus of eerie claps echoed through the court, the first sign of approval for the King's words that day.

"That confirms his guilt," declared the Queen.

"It proves absolutely nothing!" Alice protested. "You don't even understand their meaning!"

"Read them," commanded the King.

The Off-White Rabbit adjusted his spectacles. "Where shall I commence, your Majesty?" he inquired.

"Start at the beginning," the King instructed solemnly, "proceed until the end: then cease."

The Off-White Rabbit read the following cryptic verses:

"It's been one week since you looked at me
Cocked your head to the side and said, 'I'm angry'
Five days since you laughed at me
Saying, 'Get that together, come back and see me'
Three days since the living room
I realized it's all my fault, but couldn't tell you
Yesterday, you'd forgiven me
But it'll still be two days 'til I say I'm sorry

Hold it now and watch the hoodwink
As I make you stop, think
You'll think you're looking at Aquaman
I summon fish to the dish, although I like the Chalet Swiss
I like the sushi 'cause it's never touched a frying pan
Hot like wasabi when I bust rhymes

Big like LeAnn Rimes, because I'm all about value
Bert Kaempfert's got the mad hits
You try to match wits, you try to hold me but I bust through
Gonna make a break and take a fake
I'd like a stinking aching shake
I like vanilla, it's the finest of the flavors
Gotta see the show, 'cause then you'll know
The vertigo is gonna grow
'Cause it's so dangerous, you'll have to sign a waiver

How can I help it if I think you're funny when you're mad?
Trying hard not to smile, though I feel bad
I'm the kind of guy who laughs at a funeral
Can't understand what I mean? Well, you soon will
I have a tendency to wear my mind on my sleeve
I have a history of taking off my shirt

It's been one week since you looked at me
Threw your arms in the air and said, 'You're crazy'
Five days since you tackled me
I've still got the rug burns on both my knees
It's been three days since the afternoon
You realized it's not my fault not a moment too soon
Yesterday, you'd forgiven me
And now I sit back and wait 'til you say you're sorry

Chickity China, the Chinese chicken
You have a drumstick and your brain stops tickin'
Watching X-Files with no lights on

We're dans la maison
I hope the Smoking Man's in this one
Like Harrison Ford, I'm getting frantic
Like Sting, I'm tantric
Like Snickers, guaranteed to satisfy
Like Kurosawa, I make mad films, 'kay, I don't make films
But if I did they'd have a Samurai
Gonna get a set of better clubs
Gonna find the kind with tiny nubs
Just so my irons aren't always flying off the back-swing
Gotta get in tune with Sailor Moon
'Cause that cartoon has got the boom anime babes
That make me think the wrong thing"

"The pivotal evidence yet," the King interrupted, rubbing his hands; "let the jury now—"

"If any among them can decipher it," interrupted Alice, now towering and fearless, "I'll reward them handsomely. But it's all nonsensical."

The jury scribbled on their iPads, "She believes it's utter nonsense," but none dared to interpret the verses.

"If it's devoid of meaning," the King mused, "that spares us much toil, as no meaning needs to be sought. Yet," he continued, scrutinizing the verses, "I perceive some semblance of sense. '—Gotta get in tune with Sailor Moon—' You can't captain a boat, can you?" he inquired, turning to the Knave.

The Knave shook his head, a picture of misery. "I was the lone survivor of a horrifying boat accident in which 27 people drowned," he responded.

"All seems logical thus far," the King declared, continuing to mutter the verses: "'You realized it's not my fault not a moment too soon—' that refers to the jury, clearly—'You'll think you're looking at Aquaman—' that must be about me, surely—"

"But it continues 'I summon fish to the dish,'" Alice interjected.

"Ah, there they are!" the King exclaimed, pointing to the stinking plate of dead animal carcasses, among them rotting saltwater fish of various endangered species. "Nothing clearer than that. And then—'But it'll still be two days 'til I say I'm sorry,—'you've never apologized for anything, my dear?" he asked the Queen.

"Never!" the Queen snapped, hurling a bucket of lead paint at the Sewer Rat. (Poor Epstein had ceased using the iPad, as his whisker left no mark, but now frantically resumed, using the toxic pigments streaming down his face.)

"Then the verse doesn't apply to you," the King concluded, scanning the illegitimate court with a grin. A grave silence followed.

Alice desperately grabbed the Off-White Rabbit's kid glove and donned it. In her enlarged state, it barely covered a single digit.

"If the Rabbit's glove doesn't fit, you must acquit," Alice exclaimed.

The King's face turned red as his voice rose to a shout. "Let the jury deliberate their verdict," he repeated, for perhaps the twentieth time.

"No, no!" the Queen demanded. "Pronounce the sentence first—verdict after."

"Utter inhumane absurdity!" Alice bellowed. "The notion of sentencing before verdict!"

"Silence!" the Queen roared, her vascularized face turning a shade of dark violet.

"I shall not!" retorted Alice.

"Decapitate her! Live stream it!" screamed the Queen, her voice piercing the air. Yet, no one stirred.

"Who fears you?" Alice scoffed, now at her towering height. "You are merely the puppet of a ruling elite corporate class conspiring to depopulate the planet!"

At her words, everything in the courtroom surged into the air, swarming towards her with deadly velocity. Alice let out a cry, a mix of terror and rage, as she swatted at them, only to find herself in a fetal position on the bank of a long-dry river bed, her head resting in the skeletal remains of her mother's pelvis, surrounded by smoldering dead leaves.

"Wake up, Alice!" she said to herself. "You must have finally managed to sleep for several hours, undisturbed by predators."

"Oh, I've traversed such nightmarish realms in my slumber!" shouted Alice. She tried to remember surreal escapades as best as she could, but there was no one left to share them with. She hallucinated her mother's voice, remarking, "Indeed, a peculiar dream, dear: but now, hasten to drink your own urine as a last-resort means of hydration; dusk approaches and terrible dangers await you in the shadows." Thus, Alice sprang up and darted away, her mind swirling. Was this just another beam falling in the collapsing structure of her mind?

Her mother's bones lay in the dirt, motionless as Alice had left them, a desolate figure slowly turning pale under the dying sun.

Alice dwelled on her twisted and deeply disturbing adventure as a waking nightmare took hold of her, and this was the haunting vision upon which she became fatally transfixed:

In her dream, she saw herself, not with joy but as a ghostly echo, her small hands like withered leaves on her bruised and ash-stained knee, her eyes tearful and hollow, devoid of the sparkle of life. The voice she heard was not her own, but a distant, eerie whisper. The flick of her head to shift her hair seemed more the nervous tic of a lost soul roasting on a spit over the flames of Hell than an innocent child's gesture. As she listened, or thought she listened, the world around her was not vibrant but decaying, washed black in the grisly shadow of death.

The grass rustled not with life but like dry bones cast into the gutter, as the grimy Off-White Rabbit hurriedly limped by, a phantom fleeing unseen horrors. The Rat's splash in the pool was accompanied by desperate squeals and gurgles. Malt liquor bottles clinked and shattered, as the Mosquito and his friends were trapped in their never-ending, dismal binge-drinking party, under the shrill, tyrannical commands of the Queen, dooming her subjects to endless despair in a dystopian surveillance state. The juggalo baby's sneeze on the Dutchmaster's lap was stifled by methamphetamine fumes, amidst the clatter of shattered chemistry equipment. The Spider's depressing lament, the Sewer Rat's meaningless scribbling, and the choked cries of suffocating guinea-pigs filled the air, a cacophony of desolation, all underlined by the Snapping Turtle's inconsolable weeping, echoing the pervasive hopelessness of all existence.

She lingered there, eyes closed, trying to forget her residency in the desolate wasteland, knowing too well that opening her eyes would reveal the harsh truth of a colorless reality. The rustle of the dying grass would be nothing but the cold wind's whisper, the pool's ripples merely the lifeless swaying of reeds. Vibrant chatter would morph into the creaking of dead trees, the Queen's murderous cries into the distant, hollow calls of an air raid siren. The juggalo baby's "Whoop whoop", the Tapeworm's "Who the fuck are you?", and all the snot-drenched sounds of the Snapping Turtle's sobs would fade into the traumatizing soundscape of the apocalypse, with global thermonuclear explosions drowning all sound out to finality.

In the end, she pictured herself, not as a grown woman filled with warmth, but as a dehumanized shadow of herself, worn by time, holding onto the fragmented and fading memories of a childhood lost to abject desolation. She imagined her spirit dulled by the relentless passage of years, recounting tales not of wonder but of longing and loss, to dying children whose eyes reflected not eagerness but the stark emptiness of their reality. She saw herself, not finding joy, but sharing in the heavy blanket of sorrow that draped all of humanity's pathetic, wasted lives. The world before the wasteland was now nothing but a distant, mournful memory.

Acknowledgements

Thanks to Kristen and Scarlett for their love and support of my strange creative pursuits.

Thanks to Rokosz and Dirty Dog for feedback and encouragement.

Thanks to Paul for keeping the end times alive for the last twenty years.

And thanks to Mom and Dad, who I hope don't read this, for the help along the way.

About the Author

Zac Shaw has been obsessed with the disasters and the end of the world since he first grew up under the specter of global thermonuclear war in the 1980s.

He co-founded the two-piece apocalypse punk band Dead Unicorn in 2004, and is currently working on the group's sixth end-of-the-world-themed concept album, *End of the Universe.*

His eclectic projects include popular online courses, social media accounts, digital marketing, video content, journalism, web design, vintage board game and clothes vending, and a disaster-themed tabletop card game called Last Game on Earth.

Visit mediapocalypse.com for more.

Made in the USA
Middletown, DE
06 September 2024